Further praise for

"When an intriguing young woman turns up at the family's country house and strikes up a relationship with the family's matriarch, Catherine, a mystery is set in motion, lending the firmly contemporary *The Shades* a quiet echo of such classic psychological thrillers as *The Turn of the Screw* and *Rebecca*."
—Julia Vitale and Keziah Weir, *Vanity Fair*

"This psychological thriller explores the mysteries surrounding a family still reeling from profound tragedy, and the terrifying uncertainty that meets their relocation in a distant country manor."
—David Canfield, *Entertainment Weekly*

"This haunted tale follows a couple mourning the loss of their teenage daughter.... [*The Shades*] harkens back to such ghostly thrillers as du Maurier's *Don't Look Back*."
—CrimeReads

"If you're looking for a mystery to keep you on the edge of your seat, add this electrifying new novel by Evgenia Citkowitz to your reading list."
—Caroline Rogers, *Southern Living*

"Spare, arresting, and emotionally precise. A thoroughly modern novel with a Gothic feel; a fully realized vision." —*Kirkus Reviews*, starred review

"[Citkowitz's] prose sparkles as she unpacks emotional wounds.... This compact family drama captures the thinly masked desperation of grief with an eerie undercurrent." —*Publishers Weekly*

"With a deceptively light touch and an almost ethereal atmosphere, debut novelist Citkowitz delves deeply into themes of loss and grief, reality and illusion, and growth and stagnation.... [*The Shades*] is richly layered with meaning and allusions to myth and art that make it an engaging and rewarding read." —*Booklist*

"Evgenia Citkowitz's *The Shades* is not a first novel; it is a tour de force, a powerful, wicked, compassionate, and beautifully written account of the dangers we keep in our head and heart, including love. Citkowitz, a master of mood, alters our vision of what fiction is, or should be, by altering our perception of its possibilities in page after glorious page in this startling and startlingly original book."

—Hilton Als, Pulitzer Prize–winning critic and author of *White Girls*

"*The Shades* compels with searing intensity. This extraordinary myth-like novel, about a family's loss and unraveling, will live on in your imagination for a long time. Evgenia Citkowitz is a remarkable writer."

—Claire Messud, author of *The Burning Girl*

"*The Shades* is an elegant meditation on marriage, grief, and loss. In cool and beguiling prose, with a style all her own, Evgenia Citkowitz's taut and powerful novel is part mystery, part psychological portrait, and every bit engaging."

—Maria Semple, author of *Today Will Be Different* and *Where'd You Go, Bernadette*

"Evgenia Citkowitz has written a haunting novel about love and loss that moves fascinatingly back and forth across the borderlines of reality and myth. Her bold use of the cultured English upper middle class as the setting for a savage reimagining of Orpheus and Eurydice marks her out as a gifted, original writer."   —James Lasdun, author of *Afternoon of a Faun*

"*The Shades* is an elegy that reads like a fever dream of loss, a jewel box that enthralls."   —Bruce Wagner, author of *Dead Stars*

"This is a beautifully written account of how unpredictably grief operates, and how bereavement may undermine not just your contentment but your very identity. You knock back *The Shades* in a single draft. But then it kicks you in the guts."   —David Hare, creator of *Collateral* and Academy Award–nominated screenwriter of *The Hours* and *The Reader*

"I have never read a novel in which the events are recounted with such subtle interweaving back and forth through time, building up a deeply woven texture of thought and emotion. A brilliant piece of storytelling"

—Tim Pears, author of *In the Place of Fallen Leaves*

THE
SHADES

ALSO BY EVGENIA CITKOWITZ

Ether: Seven Stories and a Novella

THE
SHADES

A Novel

EVGENIA CITKOWITZ

W. W. NORTON & COMPANY
Independent Publishers Since 1923

For information about permission to reproduce selections from this book, write to
Permissions, W. W. Norton & Company, Inc., 500 Fifth Avenue, New York, NY 10110

For information about special discounts for bulk purchases, please contact
W. W. Norton Special Sales at specialsales@wwnorton.com or 800-233-4830

Manufacturing by Sheridan Books, Inc.
Book design by Michelle McMillian
Production manager: Beth Steidle

Library of Congress Cataloging-in-Publication Data

Names: Citkowitz, Evgenia, 1962– author.
Title: The shades : a novel / Evgenia Citkowitz.
Description: First edition. | New York : W. W. Norton & Company, 2018
Identifiers: LCCN 2018001584 | ISBN 9780393254129 (hardcover)
Subjects: LCSH: Psychological fiction.
Classification: LCC PS3603.I89 S53 2018 | DDC 813/.6—dc23
LC record available at https://lccn.loc.gov/2018001584

ISBN 978-0-393-35758-5 pbk.

W. W. Norton & Company, Inc., 500 Fifth Avenue, New York, N.Y. 10110
www.wwnorton.com

W. W. Norton & Company Ltd., 15 Carlisle Street, London W1D 3BS

1 2 3 4 5 6 7 8 9 0

To Julian

THE SHADES

The first and second interviews were conducted near the driveway. Her examiners were polite and serious, but they repeated back her replies as if asking more questions, obliging Catherine to reiterate her answers, creating a circular conversation that would have been absurd had not the content and the morning's events been so especially awful. With every repetition, she hoped that she wasn't beginning to sound rehearsed when she was not. Nothing could have prepared her for this surreal dialogue, and trying to account for the previous hours was challenging, as if she were suddenly required to tell a tale in a foreign dialect. Yet she remained calm. She had the feeling that she was at the end of a nightmare with an awareness that she would soon wake, but in the interim it was important to remain composed and refuse to be scared. Like the reconstituted wartime advice on a coffee mug her daughter, Rachel, had given her two Christmases back, she would keep calm and freak out later. Only after several others had come and gone to their separate conferences and huddles of activity did someone ask her if she wanted to sit down, which she interpreted as a sign of compassion. In an effort to be polite and not appear ungrateful, she accepted the offer and moved to the bench in front of the house.

Catherine took a seat and immediately felt damp rise through her skirt to the back of her thighs. It was surprising that the wooden slats still retained cold and moisture, as the location had plenty of light and exposure; recently it had been unseasonably dry with week upon week of fresh but mild late spring weather. Yet years of cool and shade seemed to have embedded in the grain, reminding her how strange it was that one piece of furniture could have become an object of continuity when all else had been subject to loss, flux, and change. This bench had been in her first flat, a basement in a Victorian terrace off Brook Green, abandoned outside by its previous owner to a snarl of brambles and untamed shrubbery, in the small apron of land that she hesitated to call a garden—the estate agent's description had been one of his more fanciful flights of marketing. After her marriage to Michael, their combined incomes had allowed them to buy the unit above, then the one over that, and turn the building once again into a single dwelling to accommodate the needs of a growing family with two young children. Once the construction was complete, Catherine turned her attention outward and started a campaign to conquer what she called her *bewilderness*. That was before she understood anything about gardening: that a north-facing aspect and the height of the boundary walls would always condemn the parterre to shade and rheumatic damp; that nothing would ever grow there except moss and more moss, but at least she had managed to reclaim the seat. When she and Michael had moved to Hamdean, Michael's *folie de grandeur* on the Weald of Kent, she'd placed it near the oak, with the idea that he would sit there at weekends—she hoped, into his dotage—to gaze in fulfillment of a lifelong obsession with houses. Only he could see the property as it had once been: an elegant Georgian manor surrounded by pristine parkland; blot out the golf course spotted with Tory retirees, and imagine they were deer grazing instead. Only he could envisage that the front portion, purchased advantageously from a bankrupt developer, was more than a façade two rooms deep, but an entire house that stretched back and beyond. That was Michael: his romance with history had always been greater than his understanding of contemporary reality. Whereas from the beginning of the project, all Catherine could see was a posh maisonette representing a separation from the family home in London, where almost three decades had passed, children had been brought up, ambitions realized, thwarted, *evolved*, and a transition to a new phase—a less fraught, more reflective one, where she and Michael could enjoy the freedoms involved with Rowan and Rachel being older. The idea had been that they would keep a base in London while the children were at school there, and on the weekends they would go to Kent—this was to be their new axis. But all this was before Rachel; before everything became the after, and the hours that passed only the enduring of them. That she ever could have conceived that Michael would be able to find peace in this spot now seemed as remote to her as his imaginary deer.

She watched the forensic workers erect a barrier and enclose the site in a tent. The crew then divided into two, with one group continuing inside and the other methodically combing the exterior. They were distinct from the regular uniformed police and plainclothes detectives. In white jumpsuits and protective clothing, their slow, mannered movements gave them the look of moonwalkers or actors in an episode of *Star Trek*. She wished she could say, *Beam me up, Scotty,* and be transported back a couple of years, away from all this mess. With a flash of irritation, she saw a photographer crouched nearby trying to get an angle of, she didn't know what, and crush a tuft of daffodils with his plastic-covered bootie. She suppressed an urge to shout, *Oi! I planted those—have some respect!*, stopping short, as she wasn't sure whether he would understand her tone, the need after a disaster to preserve what was left. She watched the spacemen walking in lines and wondered what they could possibly hope to find. She had already told detectives that it was clear that the girl had jumped off the roof: anyone could have told from her position of impossible flatness, that only a combination of gravity, velocity, and impact could have got her there. Maybe they were hoping to find a malfunctioned parachute? Or more likely, a suicide note? It was logical that they still hoped to find one. Anyone choosing to end life with such spectacular violence might well be expected to leave behind an explanation by way of dramatic follow-up. She didn't begrudge them their work. They were professionals. It was their job to look for clues, make suspicion a virtue, and labor it all. They were not Trekkies: more like archeologists of the recent past.

Catherine had been to a dig once. She was taken to Sutton Hoo by the artist John Bramley. The careful survey brought that day to mind. The site was best known for the Anglo-Saxon ship's burial of a chieftain thought to be King Raedwald, but the focus had moved to the periphery, where bodies had been discovered preserved in the sand—these were thought to be execution victims, as they were found a short distance from where the gallows had once stood. John Bramley had been dead eight years, the souls of Sutton Hoo fifteen hundred more, yet far from being ghosts, they seemed more alive and present than the girl, whom she had seen only that morning, whose body lay twenty feet away. She had known her nine or ten weeks, not yet one trimester. Was that long enough to tell? Women bonded with their children in utero in much less time. She was no daughter of hers. The girl would always be unknowable except for the damage she left behind.

"Is there anyone else here? Your husband, perhaps?" she heard a man ask.

The voice was disembodied. She refused to look to its source and acknowledge the man's presence. Her thoughts had turned to Rachel and Rowan, almost simultaneously in the same exhalation; shock had displaced her children longer than usual. She rose from the bench and headed toward the group. She didn't want to talk or answer any more questions.

Then Judith was there, flapping a blanket over her chest and shoulders. "Can't you see the state of her?" she scolded the man. "Go away."

Out of the corner of her eye, Catherine saw the inquisitor retreat.

"I'll make you tea as promised. Chamomile and nettle, dear—with something extra for the nerves."

Oh shit, she really is a witch, Catherine thought.

She had met Judith when she and Michael had first moved to Hamdean. Judith was already living in one of three apartments constructed by a developer within the original Jacobean house. Prior to conversion, the previous occupant had been the film director Clive Martin, a founding member of the British New Wave cinema, whose transition from making kitchen-sink dramas that were closer to documentary realism, to whimsical Hollywood comedies, earned him the drubbing "Quick Wave Clive" from his peers. The small manor had been built by a mercer in 1619. His office in Customs and Liveries, later Court of Wards, and profitable selling of favors, enabled him to buy ninety acres from a farmer, who'd purchased it from the Crown after its appropriation from an abbey, the ruins of which was run by a local conservancy and a local beauty spot for picnickers three miles away. Two hundred years later, a magistrate had doubled the size of the house with the addition of a façade, consisting of reception rooms, two floors of bedrooms, and an attic. He had employed an architect to lay out gardens and a deer park, "Because I cannot abide the sight of wooly sheepe." Minus elaborate topiary, and an avenue of limes that had been swept away by a furious storm forty years after planting, the basic geometry of the garden was still visible in the crosshatch lines of the kitchen garden, part of Judith's domain. Catherine found it curious that Judith occupied such a large apartment, a third of the original house, as she lived alone and was an herbalist by trade. She joked with Michael that Judith was a practitioner of the Dark Arts. One look inside her kitchen with its smoked brick inglenook, flagstones, and eternal mullioned windows, webs of washing lines draped with plants, plus a large pot (read: cauldron) boiling a soupy morass on the stove, was enough to fuel speculation that extended to their other neighbor, a financial analyst who owned the remaining apartment but was always absent, that he too was part of a cabal and a raging warlock. As to the nature of the conspiracy, the worst Catherine and Michael Francis could come up with was probably a projection of their own desires: that their neighbors were conspiring to displace them to rule house and grounds themselves. All meant to be fun, with a bit of a venal own truth thrown in. In answer to why she occupied such a large piece of real estate, Michael pointed out with some expertise, as property was his living, that it wasn't unheard-of for a nonspecialist to occasionally make a favorable deal. He had a more practical explanation for why the financial analyst was never in residence: the flat was a shell company, a tax-avoidance scheme, and the owner lived elsewhere.

Judith pulled the fleece closer to Catherine's neck. The yarn was soft and the swirls of orange and turquoise crochet were indecently bright in the gloom of the proceedings. She hadn't realized that she was cold. Gazing up at Judith, she remembered how she had once disdained her salt-and-pepper braids that looped up around her head Heidi-style, judging them ridiculous on a woman her age, but now seemed extraordinarily lovely, actually Flemish Madonna beautiful. She realized that she had been wrong about Judith, as she had been about so many things. At first glance she'd pegged her for a busybody of the kind best kept at bay. The impression had been compounded by Judith's timing. Whenever Catherine was trying to drive out pronto, to meet a train or get to an appointment, Judith would appear on the road, basket in hand, and flag her down to display her gorgeous greens culled from the wild and extol their antioxidant properties. Her neighbor's expansive view of time was so much at odds with Catherine's own that whenever she saw Judith at the newsagent's, she'd duck behind the cereal aisle to avoid a long conversation about the difficulty of finding good produce and her suspicion that all the roadside fruit stands were in fact fronts for the supermarkets.

She blinked at her.

Why had she feared her so? The dread that overfamiliarity might lead to what?—an infringement of privacy, because she lived close by? How idiotic that all seemed now.

A friendly neighbor.

Rachel alive.

The girl as well.

Those were the good old days.

Why hadn't she known it?

W hen Michael received the call from Judith, he had seen the number flashing on his mobile and assumed it was his wife telephoning from Hamdean. He had let it ring, allowing it go to voicemail. He needed a moment to adjust his thoughts away from the current preoccupation, which was not as it should have been, the survey of the Horsemead Equestrian Estate that was spread out before him on his desk. With 550 acres, one mansion, six cottages, stables, and out-buildings galore, the document had a list of dilapidations and demands from the buyer that were as excessive as the seller's taste in soft furnishings—*Berkshire brothel* was how one person in the office had described it. The same colleague had cautioned Michael that their client and seller, venture capitalist Harry Breen, was a *brinker* who would refuse to negotiate for want of a concession; that he could look forward to feverish hours while offers would be fielded and rejected, and he'd be left sweating the possibility of a lost commission. But Michael had enough experience dealing with the shrewdly wealthy (as opposed to the stupidly wealthy—there was a difference) to know that Breen's arrogance and willingness to walk could work in their favor and get them all what they wanted. Besides, the package was stunning. It was in the Cotswolds, with a scale and setting so gorgeous that he might as well be selling fields of manna or gold. Thankfully this type of high-end sale still existed, as it had helped him keep his head above financial quicksand. Low and average properties were tethered by market forces; extraordinary ones floated in bubbles above, unpunctured by spiking interest rates and pernicious mortgage-backed securities. In normal circumstances, the survey in question would have been read by him even before it touched his inbox, but it had actually lain there for two days unread. Earlier his assistant, Karen, had walked past and patted the folder as a tactful way of reminding him that massage duties on the deal were currently overdue. In the moments before he heard the phone ringing, and honestly a good part of the previous forty-eight hours, Michael had not been thinking about the million-pound shortfall conditioned by oligarch Dmitri Dhokhorov's offer, he had been thinking about himself and his own personal ground plan that looked bleak and sketchy.

Swiveling his chair, he looked out the window that bowed over the city, thirty floors high. He did that whenever he had a problem to solve. His office had a view that never failed to impress, and helped mitigate the choices he'd made when he'd left the conservation department at English Heritage to work at Great Estates. Whenever he looked out at the interlapping roofs, a patchwork of existence expressed in architectural form, from the pinnacle of Wren to a surgical sheath of glass and iron jutting up next door, he saw a story of growth: that each build-ing had emerged in spite of the next, monuments to the best and worst of human endeavor, feats of engineering and imagination just the same. He always said that looking at the skyline could clarify his thoughts, with the distance giving him a fresh per-spective by elevating him from his cares below.

Today there was no solution in his sights, only a vision of the aspects of his life that were broken. *Fucked.* He disliked pro-fanity, as it was crude and imprecise, but *fucked* suddenly popped into his head and seemed so much more expressive than any other description he could summon. Such thoughts were unfa-miliar and undermined him; positivity wasn't a mood but a precept of character. He had endured fourteen months of hell but still had managed to fulfill his obligations as a father, hus-band, and professional. He had never claimed to be the world's best at anything, but at least he had known to value common sense and judgment above weakness and error. Yet, after one of the most challenging weekends, he'd come home from the office and, when least expecting, had a conversation that had begun innocently enough, then left him destabilized and wanting.

Paige Wells had telephoned the flat looking for Catherine. Paige was one of Catherine's oldest friends from uni, although the decades had subjected their bonds to some of the attenua-tions of time. For over twenty years he'd heard a variation on the theme of Paige: Paige was the greatest. Paige could be full of herself. Once she became the successful editor of a woman's glossy, Paige was a blowhard. "She talks at you. She thinks she's dictating an angle for a magazine article without stopping to listen to the feedback." There had been some further estrangement between them over Paige's attitude toward a young woman whom Catherine had wanted to help, but he hadn't had the mental energy to understand what had happened, or to adjudicate who had been right and who had been wrong. Yet, when her bossy ex–best friend had telephoned the flat looking for Catherine, she had stayed on the line and they had talked for a while. Contrary to her reputation, she was sympathetic and kind.

Paige was worried that Catherine hadn't been returning her calls. "She's isolating, Michael. That can't be good. I don't know what I can do if she won't talk to me." He had the same concerns—and more. Yet, knowing that the two women had some issues between them, he listened and said as little as possible, as he didn't want to aggravate the situation between two friends. Paige asked how he was, and he couldn't answer because he didn't know—all he could think to talk about was an incremental rise in the market, the day's penthouse viewing in Hyde Park, and the surprise of finding a naked man in the kitchen. She countered by admitting to the brain damage of lunch with advertisers, the boredom of which had compelled her to go to the bathroom mid-course, to read the gossip pages on her mobile, and then in a *moral expunging* read "Burnt Norton" on a poetry app. The effect of these minor confessions was cheering; the easy inconsequentiality of their banter had an intimacy that he realized he was craving and made him yearn for something more. He would have liked to have prolonged their dialogue with something other than husky admissions, such as inviting her over with the intention of doing something shameless, but that was ludicrous, so he left the idea where it belonged: as a silly, juvenile fantasy.

After decades of fidelity these impulses were disturbing, as it left him exposed, but this wasn't entirely bad, as it forced him to assess himself and confront some difficult questions. After an epic night alone, he had been forced to stare down the fall lines of his marriage to Catherine. He had seen how they had clung to each other out of fear and habit, and wondered whether it was time to let go and jump—the unknown abyss was looking a lot more preferable to the purgatory he was in. Much as he had tried not to dwell on emotions aroused the previous day, as they were distracting from the bigger picture—whatever that was—although images of Paige's ripe limbs and aubergine hair kept coming back to him and were probably all the more delicious for being forbidden, he had surrendered to lustful thoughts in the early hours, hoping that they didn't constitute lechery or betrayal. At 4:10 a.m. he got up and made himself porridge.

Looking out over the city, he realized that the deterioration of his relationship with Catherine was about as unsurprising as the demolition of the shipper's warehouse next door that he'd watched being torn down over several days. There was a momentum to these things: once the wrecking ball was in motion it was near impossible to stop. Few would mourn what had been there before and only what had taken its place would seem to matter. He hoped that Catherine would catch up to these feelings, since she had been the one driving them, unconsciously or not. While Paige was right to say that Catherine had become isolated, there had also been encouraging signs of late—her renewed interest in others had been a major one. When he had last seen Catherine two days before, she had been at her most argumentative and confrontational, but she was also the most fiercely energetic that he had seen in fourteen months. It was more than possible that she was on the way to getting back to being the formidable Catherine of old.

Perhaps the most unlikely sensation at that moment was the lightness in his chest, almost a fluttering, as if a host of butterflies had been trapped and would soon burst forth in a surge of optimism. He saw obstacles ahead but had a presentiment that he could overcome them; if he'd been asked a day before, he would have said he would not. He had survived the worst of years, running flagellating circles of self-recrimination, but he was still alive and there was nothing else to do except keep moving forward and living. The idea of preserving the status quo was too bleak to ponder.

He allowed his imagination to take flight over this new terrain and pictured what life might look like in a Catherine-free zone.

He saw himself looking for a flat. They'd have to sell Hamdean first—not good in a soft market, and it was too particular for a quick sale. When he had bought the place, the price had already been knocked down; he had paid more for it than he should, having factored years of use into the equation.

He'd have to move out of central London, as rents would be too high. The thought of that depressed him. He could see that he'd have to be proactive about making new relationships, as it didn't suit him to be alone. It was unlikely that anything romantic would develop at work—he and his colleagues barely tolerated one another by day—whatever brief thoughts he'd had about Paige, she was eliminated by virtue of her friendship with Catherine, while allowing for images of her with her poetry app in the bathroom stall of a fashion magazine.

He hovered for a moment, wondering where men of a certain age went to meet people.

Bar, theater, concert?

Starbucks?

After that it was a slippery slope to the Internet.

His spirits sagged. The landscape with difficult Catherine looked more alluring than the great unknown.

Most seriously, he saw that Catherine wasn't as strong as he would like to believe. Although optimism was important, she was still fragile; he wasn't sure how she'd be able to cope on her own. He was ashamed that he'd entertained such disloyalty. He felt foolish that he had been naïve enough to think that he could excise the flesh wound of history, plaster himself with a Band-Aid, and be healed in time for a serendipitous meeting at Wagamama. This wasn't who he was: a dastardly quitter who shied from responsibility. He always did the right thing. He wasn't going anywhere; he cared too much about Catherine. He would never leave.

The belief that he still had stamina and purpose marked a return to form, as his life had always been governed by a steady diligence—dogged could have been Michael's middle name. In this respect he was more like his parents than he liked to admit. When he was old enough for entry as a day boy, his father had taken a position at St. Christopher's, a private school in Hampshire, remaining there thirty years, a soft-spoken fixture of the history department. This unassuming figure had managed a Herculean task of shoring up five successively inadequate headmasters, until the last in the chain of incompetents forced his retirement at the age of fifty-eight. The gold pen he was given for long service was to sit on his desk barely used, apart from the occasional writing of shopping lists and condolence letters to bereaved friends. Fifteen years later his penmanship was fondly remembered by one such recipient of his kind sentiments, in a letter to his widow after his death. Michael's mother had trained as an elementary schoolteacher, but opted for an administrative position at St. Chris's, as a family with two employees qualified for better housing in the form of a *really very nice* bungalow, almost in bowling distance of the cricket pitch. This feature came into play when Michael was quarantined with chicken pox and could watch games standing on the table with a pair of binoculars. However, simple home economics meant that while other students summered and wintered in other locations, Michael's holidays were spent on school grounds—either alone in the library or kicking around an empty soccer field, playing a solitary waiting game, knowing he had no choice but to slog it out. He had no brothers or sisters for company, although he picked up fairly quickly that his mother had wanted another child, hearing her being asked by other mothers how many children she had. Her response was always terse. *Just the one,* she said, sometimes adding, *two wasn't meant to be* and rearing her head as he'd seen horses do. It wasn't difficult for him to read disappointment into her gestures; like him, she too had taken the short straw.

Michael's industriousness continued all the way to university, where he'd taken a history scholarship at Christ Church, and lasted through his marriage, which had always been hard work, with him doing more than his share of the heavy lifting. He had met Catherine at a saleroom viewing. He had stopped at the auction house on the way to deliver a letter for his boss. She was one in a phalanx of polished assistants at the ready, armored with ambition and smarts. He noticed her immediately: her proud nose and jaw, eyes guarded by fierce intelligence. When he asked a question about the provenance of a group of architectural drawings, her detailed and specific knowledge of drafting techniques and paper conservation made it quickly apparent that she was the cleverest person in the room. He had to return several times before summoning the nerve to ask her out for coffee. When he did, she was up-front that she didn't want a relationship. She had just moved to London, she explained. To stay afloat she had to put all her energy into work. In any case, she warned, she wasn't good company. Her mother had died suddenly while she was away finishing her master's. Six months later she was only just beginning to process what had happened—the circumstances around her mother's death were never clear. He appreciated that she was honest about the more painful aspects of her family's history. The candor of her rejection only deepened his interest by making him understand the need for patience; otherwise he would not have lasted through the next two dates, which were a torture—she was distant and aloof and he couldn't help being stiff and boring. However, on the third date, he managed to penetrate her indifference. On a lucky hunch, he had bought tickets to a concert performance of Monteverdi's *L'Orfeo*—the fact the tickets were cheap had been as much a motivating factor as an interest in early Baroque music.

The opera, written in Italian, retold the mythic story of Orpheus's journey to the underworld to bring back his wife, Eurydice, after her death. When Orfeo tries to cross the Styx, the river that separates the land of the living from the dead, Caronte, ferryman of shades, the souls of the dead, refuses to take him, as Orfeo is still alive. Orfeo uses all his art to serenade him to sleep before making the passage across. Once

Orfeo is reunited with his beloved wife, his mission fails after
he breaks the one condition that has been imposed on him by
Pluto: on leaving Hades he must not look back. In contrast to
other versions that had Orpheus torn apart by Maenads, female
worshipers of Dionysus, in Monteverdi's *L'Orfeo* the lovers are
given a triumphant reprieve when Apollo intervenes and whisks
them up to heaven.

The music was astonishing. The lack of costumes or sets
didn't diminish the power of the performances. Sitting close
to Catherine and listening to sublime expressions of loss and
yearning, while attuned to the rise and fall of her breath, was its
own ecstatic experience. During the impasse between Orfeo and
Caronte at the Styx, hearing the ferryman's stark *basso* refusal,
Michael saw there were tears rolling down the side of her face.
He offered his hand, which she took, interlacing her fingers
between his. The clasp was intimate, charged by something
more than friendship. After, they walked toward the under-
ground station, chatting unreservedly as they joined the throng
of people emptying from theaters and pubs. They were plugged
in, connected to each other. At that moment, with the energy
surging between them, he could have believed that all the people
around them were part of the same electrical network too. She
was effusive in her praise for *L'Orfeo*. "It's pure, unfettered by
character or needless plot—totally modern."

Michael found this refreshing to hear of something written
in 1609. "Yes, it's often described as the first opera—or the
first to have been considered worth writing down. It must have
seemed very *d'avanguardia* back then."

"It's groundbreaking now. It doesn't stop being modern just because it has been copied." She stopped. "I'm sorry if I was a baby in there. It was the ferryman's voice. It wasn't human—more like a foghorn, a warning in the dark."

"No apology necessary." Then, because she was so serious, he added, "Just as well we saw the version with the happier ending."

"It isn't about whether he was successful in bringing her back," she corrected, "it's that he went to get her at all."

This seemed to him as good a definition of love as any, and moved him to lean in and kiss her. As her response was kinetic, they hopped in a taxi and went directly to her digs in Bermondsey, to have sex in the bathroom of her roommate's flat.

Their relationship proceeded much as he intended, as if all boxes were being ticked. Within four years Michael had persuaded her to marry him. Yet, there was something else in the margins, a remoteness that created a space between them that he never understood; except, bottom line, he knew that his attentions were not quite reciprocated. He noticed that their lives ran parallel but never together or intersecting, and that was what he longed for and missed, some collision of purpose. They had art in their lives. As much as he loved old masters, he did not share her passion for abstraction, or her desire to be out every night looking at it. She found his taste for museum collections fusty, and said there was nothing more stifling than an object or painting behind glass. Then there were children—but curiously this had not brought them together. She made all the decisions and he always felt relegated to the role of a benign onlooker rather than active co-parent.

Then Rachel was dead. After that, time had staggered and crawled, with each day as heavy and insurmountable as the next. Although after the accident he was bonded in grief with Catherine, their interchanges soon went back to being little more than a scheduling of movements that were designed for her to be in one place while he was in another; now that there were two homes, this was easier to manage. Catherine chose the country to be nearer Rowan's school, while he preferred to be in London because he could always cry work as a reason not to be there— meeting only highlighted their insufficiencies and reminded them both of failure. Soon after, Rowan was gone as well.

In many ways they had taken him for granted. He was born within a year of Rachel—*Irish twin*, Catherine had said, hearing she was pregnant again—but unlike his sister, for whom everything was an imperative and nothing was accomplished without a dramatic statement of it, Rowan had a relaxed, even temperament. They never worried about him as he breezed through his school subjects, allowing them to believe lack of stress was a measure of stability and success. Rowan was a natural middle-distance runner with an athletic style that was as effortless as his academic approach. His coaches gave up trying to correct his lolloping gait because he was unbeatable and a marvel to watch because he made the 1500m look so goddamn easy. He was the team's star runner but turned down the captaincy, as he had an innate dislike of bureaucracy; he had no desire to send nanny-mails about uniforms and race-day breakfasts. If the pedestrian traffic at the house in London on weekends was any indication, he had no shortage of friends, male and female. After Rachel's death, they entered unfamiliar territory together, but when they looked to their son he was already distancing himself, receding still, leaving them in an even more lonely and inhospitable place.

The call had come in the early hours of the morning; the kind any parent lived to dread. The officer provided few details. He would tell Michael only that his daughter had been involved in a motor accident: she was in Chelsea and Westminster A&E. Michael had been traced through the mobile found in her pocket by dialing the number in the address book marked "Dad." On the way to the hospital Catherine unraveled. She reproached herself for having allowed Rachel to stay with a friend from school, Mira, whom they barely knew; for not having taken the time to ask basic questions about where Rachel was going, what she was doing. She had only a superficial impression of Mira and her parents from seeing them at a fund-raiser, the mother with the soulful kholed eyes and expensive handbag. She didn't even know where the family lived. Michael kept telling her, *She's going to be all right. She's going to be all right*, as if by persuading them both he could affect the outcome.

By the time they arrived, they were already too late: their daughter had been dead ten minutes. They heard that the cause of death was a subdural hematoma, as she'd been partially ejected from the car. They were told that the driver had also been killed instantly: both air bags had failed to activate. Neither passenger had been wearing a seat belt. Alcohol had been found on the floor, so there was the question of whether the driver had been drinking. The other party involved—a van driver—was in intensive care. He later testified that the other car had been going eighty miles per hour and jumped the light, blindsiding him as he made a protected green-arrow right turn. Further investigation of CCTV footage corroborated this view.

All this was told by Jackie, a pale crisis worker, with the tact and delicacy of a practiced bearer of bad news, with the officer who had telephoned Michael standing by. After hearing the worst, Catherine said, "Rachel couldn't drive. She didn't have a license. Nor did Mira. They were too young, you see." She'd managed a smile, although the stream of anguished tears told another story. However, the social worker cautioned that Catherine should prepare herself as they'd found an ID belonging to Rachel in the car. The police officer added that the vehicle— a *Porsche*—he said significantly, was registered to the name of Merhan Azadi, and it appeared that he had been the driver.

"I don't understand." Catherine had stared at him blankly.

But Michael did. He always remembered a name, face or place. "Azadi is her family's name. Our daughter's friend. The driver must have been her father."

"More like her brother, sir," the officer suggested. "The driver was seventeen." Soon after, they learned that his supposition was right.

They were taken to see her, already a waxen image, a poor, damaged effigy of their child. The social worker had left them alone, but the sight had sickened Michael as if his body were trying to reject the terrible information he was being forced to ingest. When Catherine broke down—he was surprised that she had managed to hold up so long—Michael was glad to take her out and get away from this cruel imposter, the travesty of their daughter, and the noxious smell of antiseptic that was no match for the pervading one of death.

As they left, they saw a couple coming toward them in the corridor. Almost a mirror image of themselves. Bent in grief, shrouded in tears. They were being escorted by bloodless Jackie, who was working double shifts and proving to be the Caronte of the Chelsea and Westminster. Michael immediately recognized the couple. Like Catherine, he remembered Mrs. Azadi's luminous eyes, all the more distinct for being the only part of her that wasn't swathed in scarves or clothing, but now looked up at them in clouded red half moons. At the sight of Catherine, she stood up straight, as if seeing another woman who was mad with grief had suddenly made her stronger. She said, "Mrs. Francis—" She broke off; she couldn't find anything else to say.

"Please tell me why Rachel wasn't at home with Mira." Catherine's voice was restricted, as if someone were squeezing her throat.

Mr. Azadi replied, "She went for a drive with Merhan. That's all." His tone was abrupt and defensive; Michael might have said a little rude.

Catherine stiffened. "That wasn't the plan. You know that wasn't the plan." Her voice had dropped and become firm. Michael observed she was preternaturally calm.

"They were young. Young people go out. You can't follow them around, checking on every single thing they do," Mr. Azadi responded dismissively.

Jackie, seeing the situation was deteriorating, jumped in. "Mrs. Francis, we should all take time to gather our—"

Catherine ignored Jackie, directing more questions at Mr. Azadi. "May I ask how long your son had been driving?"

"Two months," he answered, adding, "he was a very good driver."

Catherine snorted, "When you gave your seventeen-year-old a fast car, seriously, what did you expect?"

Her sudden, prosecutorial stance took everyone by surprise. The Azadis gasped. Michael did the same, quickly intervening, "We're all in shock. We shouldn't be having this conversation."

Jackie agreed, "You all need time to—"

But Mr. Azadi dismissed her with his hand, his chest swelling with outrage, "My son was a gentleman. They were in love and planning to be married."

"Oh, for God's sake. You think they were Diana and Dodi, do you? And that makes it okay?" Catherine made that snorting sound again.

"How dare you insult me at such a time? My son is dead."

"But your daughter is alive."

There was a stunned quiet before Mrs. Azadi sobbed, "Take me to see him. *Mojan, Mojan.*" Her cry seemed to startle her husband out of his anger. Embracing his wife, Mojan Azadi turned her away from the offending sight, nodding to Jackie to continue on their course. Jackie hurried in front of them, leaning in as she walked, presumably to comfort the stricken woman. Michael heard Mr. Azadi utter something in Farsi, before calling back, "When you mocked his memory, you also mocked your daughter. What kind of woman are you?"

Michael saw Catherine was going to answer again but stopped her this time. "No, Catherine. No."

Jackie led the Azadis down the corridor. Outside the room where Michael and Catherine had just seen Rachel, they turned and entered the room across the hall.

It wasn't long before Catherine began to regret the ugly scene: a matter of minutes. After seeing their destination, she was able to calm herself. She said she hadn't been in control; something about Mr. Azadi's arrogance and lack of apology, had triggered her into becoming a vengeful and cruel person who wanted to see him punished. She didn't need Michael to point out how unfortunate the situation had been, or how badly she had behaved, so he didn't comment, listening quietly to her expressions of sorrow and remorse while suppressing his own. In the days that followed she had a keen urge to see Mira and her family. She wanted to talk to them, find out how Rachel had been on the last day of her life. She wanted to know if there had been anything between Rachel and Merhan. Mr. Azadi's accounting of their relationship wasn't enough; she wanted to know more—no detail would have been too small. The idea that Rachel had experienced some sort of love or affection before her death now seemed beautiful for being brief and fragile. She wrote letters asking forgiveness to Mr. and Mrs. Azadi. These were returned unopened. The flowers that she sent were also returned the same day. Catherine's behavior at the hospital had inflicted untold damage on everyone, but there was no one she had hurt more than herself.

Michael Francis stared through the window. The buildings seemed less triumphant, compromised by their aggressive proximity. Even the newer ones seemed to have lost their sheen.

He saw the voicemail icon flashing and wondered what Catherine could be wanting. It was unusual for her to use the office number and call so late in the afternoon.

Catherine was outside Hamdean when she first saw the girl. A red BMW deposited her, made a quick U-turn, and drove off at such a speed that Catherine thought that if she was ever to see that car again she would be sure to give its idiot driver a bollocking. From a distance, she sized up the young woman: slight but not athletic, rounded shoulders, poor posture—apparently, no one had ever told her that she needed to stand up straight. Her dark, choppy hair was pushed back in an Alice band and tufted up behind. No sleek, amber mane. The girl didn't seem to register her, but instead rummaged inside her bag to find sunglasses and put them on, raising her head in the general direction of the house. The bag she carried was the same slouchy, unstructured kind that Rachel liked, although this hadn't always been her taste. When Rachel was eight, she had become attached to a stiff '50s snap purse that had belonged to Catherine's mother and had refused to go anywhere without it. Catherine remembered the age it took for her to assemble its contents: crayons, plastic animal—usually a horse—some kind of snack (this would be negotiated), before she was ready to make a gap-toothed promenade, her ladylike accouterment swinging over one small arm.

She turned away, wishing that Judith would give her patients better directions so they did not come by and bother her. This was precisely why she didn't like going out.

That morning Catherine had moved twenty stacks of mail from the dining room, where it had been sitting, an unwanted visitor, to the kitchen, where it could no longer be avoided or ignored. The sight of so many unopened letters was daunting, as each one represented an unspoken demand. Michael had offered to come down to help, but she had insisted on leaving it to do in her own time. It was important to hang on to the last semblance of competence. Besides, she had become accustomed to being alone. She made a cup of Judith's muddy tea, ignoring complex brewing instructions, dunking the pouch, chucking it away. She managed a surprisingly efficient pre-sort, soon determining that most of the mail was junk and could be tossed without opening. Personal correspondence was easily identified. She recognized the determined hand of Paige, doubtless full of intention and useless prescription. There was little chance that Catherine would get involved with another foundation, take up meditation, tai chi or Zumba. Anything that looked as though it might contain a condolence was put aside to be opened at some future date. As she had discovered, sympathy did nothing for her. She didn't need it, nor did she want it. She also made a start on her electronic backlog, pulling up pages upon pages of unopened bold that seemed to glare out at her. Reproach from her inbox was mutual: she resented the messages for presuming on her at a time when she had no interest in reading them. She made a decision that emails could wait another day. Now that contact had been reduced to essentials—everyone who mattered knew to telephone (or in Rowan's case, text), and Lewis called only when there was something that she absolutely needed to know—this pared down existence, the habit of ignoring anything extraneous was beginning to seem like an economical use of time.

As she hadn't been to the gallery in months, it was just as well that most of her business had devolved upon the administration of artists' estates, with only one group show planned for later in the year. It was also good that Lewis had become so adept at keeping it all going in her absence. One of her better decisions was turning out to have been the hiring of Lewis, the son of a prominent American literary agent who had transplanted to London. Lewis had been raised in the UK and was now indistinguishable from any young Englishman who had been to Stowe and the London School of Economics, having turned from a career in economics to art with the realization that the two were not mutually exclusive. He was subtle and polite, persuasive but not pushy. She had once observed him with a collector looking at a Camden School gouache, and credited him for knowing exactly what to say: something scholarly about Matisse's découpées, followed by something subjective, and she'd liked the way he'd known to withdraw in a timely manner, allowing the collector to bond with the picture and fall in love. Being front man suited Lewis. He was making it easier for her to opt out, and he was benefiting from the exchange.

That she would have left the gallery to a subordinate for more than one week would have been inconceivable at any time before the accident. Having devoted twenty years to a business that manifested a vision of what was relevant and mattered, she managed every detail and left nothing to chance. No one else could have replicated her interaction with artists and clients, which was always specific and direct. In terms of her professional development, certain relationships were more significant than others. No association had been more formative or important to her than with the artist John Bramley.

She had been sent to see him by her boss, Jay Katz, to check progress on five paintings that were overdue for delivery. She was a novice then, having worked at Katz Inc. only two months, hired straight from the front desk at Christie's, where she had been seated after finishing her master's—Jay had told her he'd recognized in her the look of a hungry cub. She considered herself lucky to have been given the task, even knowing all the different levels of responsibility the visit involved. There was pleasing Katz, a maverick on the contemporary art scene, whose entry to London from New York and brash pricing was causing unrest amongst his competitors in Cork Street; there was satisfying herself, unlikely by her own exacting standards; and there was impressing the artist, a formidable talent but an unknown quantity personally—all she knew about the man was that he'd been married three times. His first wife had left him for another woman, his second, for his first dealer. She didn't know much about his third wife, also an artist, said to have been very beautiful until her looks were ravaged by alcohol. At the time of Catherine's visit, John's work had been undervalued in the marketplace, but perception of him was quickly changing thanks to representation by Katz and entry into key collections, resulting in rapid leaps in the prices he commanded.

She was two hours late for the meeting: road works and a ten-mile tailback had turned the drive to his Suffolk cottage into a constipated crawl. In her apologies to the master she never could bring herself to admit that she'd added another thirty minutes to the journey, circling a labyrinth of un-signposted lanes and hedgerows, wishing she had been sensible enough to bring a map. He lived on a working farm, not unlike her parents' home in Sussex, only Catherine's father, a potter, had converted all the outbuildings to make a compound for local craftsmen and had rented the fields to a neighbor for grazing. Sweet hay and rancid silage were the smells of childhood, but the familiarity did little to soothe nerves aggravated by the journey.

John Bramley was polite to the point of courtliness, pulling up a chair, offering refreshment with the clipped articulations of a Cambridge education. He regarded her with a stark curiosity that bordered on concern, but it didn't take long for her to realize that he wasn't severe but serious. When he invited her to eat supper—he'd been cooking lamb on a greasy Aga when found—Catherine was bold enough to ask to see his studio. He handed her boots (*size 5: wife number three?*) for the march across a sodden field to a corrugated metal–clad structure, fitted with skylights that must have been a hay barn once. Inside were four large abstract landscapes, executed with dark, gestural swathes that seemed to sweep all the terror and beauty of existence into the impasto. No less powerful than the big-scale canvases, was a small oil sketch of lilting rhomboids that drew her attention. Outlined in graphite, three alabaster forms floated on a pale field of striated gray. Unlike the angst and turmoil of the other pieces, the image was magnetically serene. However, the sun was lowering—the artist only worked in natural light—there was no electricity, only a wood-burning stove; Bramley made it clear that he was unhappy for her to look at his paintings in this way. They returned to his cottage and drank some good Burgundy while eating an aromatic stew. He plied her with questions. What kind of man was her partner? ("A good one.") Were they planning to marry? ("We're on track.") The conversation turned to Constable, Matisse, Gauguin, and his transition from portraiture to expressionism. He caught her off guard by asking why Katz hadn't come to see him himself. The truth was that her boss had stayed behind to receive a collector who was circling a knockout Bacon, a newly discovered version of *The Buggers*. The owner of the picture, a friend of Francis's and regular of the Colony Room, had been persuaded by the wily dealer to release it for a condition report, giving Jay Katz five days to come up with an over-the-odds, irresistible offer before the picture had to be returned. The gallerist knew from experience that when people were separated from their possessions they were most susceptible to cash offers. He had already lined up three punters: one duke, one government minister, and the manager of a rock band who was likely to trump them both.

At first Catherine had tried to cover for her boss—"Jay is truly sorry that he has been detained in London"—before opting for a more direct approach, with omissions. "He doesn't know if you're working, and that worries him. So here I am. I came instead." She'd sounded more upbeat than she'd intended.

"And he thinks you will magically beguile me into producing more than I have?"

"No, of course not," she'd said, mortified that he would think she would be so crass, although fine with the perception that Katz might be. "I can only tell you that I will do my utmost to support your immense talent and see it properly represented."

She was relieved that he didn't contradict her credo.

"If Katz has become fat and indolent," he said, "I hope the condition has not affected his eyes." With that, he'd raised his glass to her. She was glad to see that he was smiling.

He asked her to stay, but she declined, retreating instead to the discomfort of a concave mattress at the local B&B, to spend the night wondering whether she'd been presumptuous about the nature of his invitation—maybe all he'd been offering was a decent bed? The next morning he'd telephoned her early. Instead of returning to the studio, he wanted to show her a place of "greater significance." He picked her up and drove her ten miles to Sutton Hoo, where an excavation had been in progress, intermittently, since 1939.

The site seemed to lie in supplication to the sky; skinless and exposed with its topsoil scraped away. Most of the burial mounds had been restored and allowed to grass over once again, while those still under examination gaped open like cystic wounds. Bramley was a familiar on the scene. He was on first-name terms with archeologists and researchers alike and afforded the privilege of circulating unsupervised. With one hand on Catherine's elbow, the other daubing the direction of points of interest, he guided her around while speaking of the venerable Miss Pretty, who had owned the land and lived in the austere white house across the field. Miss Pretty had been interested in spiritualism. After hearing reports of supernatural activity in the area, she had funded the first excavation that yielded the monumental discovery of King Raedwald's ship, with its trove of chattels and treasures. When John had taken her to see the grim figures of the sand men, where they lay hunched and undefended in their pits—like those caught in the molten lava of Vesuvius, they looked as though they might have been buried alive—she'd had the impression that he was posing some sort of question by bringing her there, but was at loss to know what it was. He seemed to intuit her thoughts: "I come here often to visit my neighbors, the ones that came before. Each hill and rut belongs to them and echoes with their call. They remind me what it means to be alive." His connection with the ancient dead was startling: equally, the clarity with which he seemed to be looking at his own mortality, even challenging it with a willful stare. As she stood by, the rhomboid abstract that she had glimpsed in his studio came to her, allowing her to understand what the image represented: a preoccupation with places of interment, past, present, future. For Catherine, the insight was profound, so disarming, that she stepped back, as if she were to stay too close to the trench's edge, she might be propelled down there in the direction of his gaze. That he had revealed himself to her was an act of trust, a vote of confidence that braced an eighteen-year bond. She went on to co-curate one more show for him with Katz, then another independently as his sole dealer. Her final tribute to John Bramley was the organization of a museum retrospective, fulfilling the promise she had made to him the day that they met.

She had been warned about the first anniversary, that it was a mistake to think that it would push her one day further away from her loss, when it would only bring her one day closer to its permanence. It wasn't until the weekend after the first anniversary of Rachel's death that the cold weight of this eternity had flattened her. By force of will, she had made herself get up before she surrendered to the silence.

There were different kinds of quiet. Not all bad. There was the fertile kind of artists, which she knew from studio visits and enjoyed. She liked the economy of speech, that words came from seeing; conversation only happened when there was something to say. Silence was always productive: full of ideas and crowded with consciousness. John Bramley was famously taciturn. Over the years he'd unnerved many a sitter. Although in the evening, in the company of friends, when work was done and his brushes were down, he would exhale and expand like the Burgundy in his decanter, and become confidential and downright talkative.

Her father was the same when he was making. He didn't speak much or waste time with small talk or chatter. When Catherine appeared in the shed, he'd hand her a lump of clay in lieu of conversation, and hours would pass while she watched him etching and molding, making glazes that were alchemical in their ability to fire from dull colors into iridescent hues, with barely a word passing between them—and that was fine too. Once, seeing her anticipation, he cautioned her that for all his experience he still never could be sure that a ceramic would survive a double firing. Sometimes, for reasons unknown—air pressure, water quality, mineral composition of the clay—a piece would emerge from the kiln fissured or broken. He likened the pale bisque-ware on the shelf, lined up for passage through the infernal heat, to souls waiting for a chance of eternity. These variables aside, he told her that art only happened when labor, intention, and craft came together. "You can toil all you want and the object of your attention is ugly, but with one brave turn it can become rare and beautiful. To an outsider that looks like a flick of the wrist, but I warrant you, it's not."

In spite of all the hours spent in the studio receiving so many wisdoms, she developed no talent for the medium and did little more than toy with the clay—his processes were far more interesting to watch. She did like to coil and made legions of snails. "Another escargot?" he'd ask, indulging her, and she'd nod and set about making yet another pinwheel mollusk. Only when she reached a precocious eleven did she force questions about his pottery that was mostly sold in gift shops. How much did a tea set cost to make? How much did he charge? She noted that one teapot was really three pieces by the time he'd made the body, attached the handle, made the lid—then there were those pesky cups. Why didn't he make a jug or vase that would be quicker, then he could make and sell more? She'd observed with some anxiety that money was tightly parsed.

Her father laughed, praising her acumen. Taking a lumpen mass of clay to the wheel, he raised a cylinder, as only a conjuror could do.

"Our experiment, dear girl—big enough for flowers. A *Catherine Jug*. What color should it be?"

"Blue," she'd replied.

"What shade? Be more exact."

"Anything but navy." She'd smacked the box pleats of an offending uniform skirt.

"What would you have against navy?"

"Boring."

He allowed the wheel to slow to a halt.

"Ah, no mystery. I agree it appears a little solid. Color comes from light. What you see depends on how many wavelengths the object can absorb or reflect and send back to the eye."

"You mean the color isn't there?" This information was disorienting, as it flipped her understanding of the physical world on its head.

"That brain of yours decides. Do you think gray could pass muster?"

"Only if it has blue in it."

"The mist."

With a deft press of his thumb, a spout appeared on the rim.

"You're not alone in your passion," he continued. "Centuries ago, people crossed seas, climbed the mountains of Afghanistan to find precious stones of lapis lazuli to grind into pigment to make the most profound and sacred of blues, *ultramarine.*"

"Was it expensive?"

"More valuable than gold, because it was rare and prized by all the master painters."

He slid a piece of wire under the jug, neatly slicing it from the turntable. "Are there any other blues you'd find acceptable?" His voice was clipped. She sensed that he hadn't liked her question.

"The sky when it's sunny, the sea in photos when it's clear, baby blue and turquoise rings . . ."

When Rachel was born her eyes were blue, but turned brown. Rowan's were the same, then a curious gray, flecked with moss green. *Irish twin.* Why did she ever think that was funny?

Her father started calling her *Manager Catherine*, which she didn't find as amusing as he seemed to do, but she was pleased when she heard that the jug had sold for the same price as the more labor-intensive tea set.

Then there was her mother's silence that began after the episode—a chill that hardened into a freeze, fragile enough to shatter at any moment.

Rosemary Hall hadn't always been so brittle.

As a younger woman, she was mild and conscientious. She managed the farm and the family's tenuous finances, supervising Catherine's homework, attentive to the details, the minutiae of her needs—she was emphatic that her daughter should work hard to succeed academically, to qualify herself to enter any field of interest she desired. The only hint of the forecast might have been her mother's hovering air of anxiety, but as she lived in perpetual wait, whether for rent from tenants who never paid on time—like her husband they were artisans, surviving sale by sale—or for her husband to emerge, to receive pieces that would be packed carefully in newspaper and loaded into the shuddering Morris Minor for distribution around local gift shops, a certain apprehensiveness could have been perfectly natural. That her mother was capable of a singularly destructive act, at first sight seemed not just unlikely, but impossible.

The episode in question involved a commission from Kitty Lisle, widow of the Liberal MP Sir Richard Lisle, who owned an Elizabethan jewel house and garden on the West Sussex–Surrey border. Mrs. Lisle, previously of Cape Town, and married to one of the directors of De Beers, had cultivated an interesting sculpture garden of Moore, Hepworth, and Caro at Rother Park, with a small but choice collection of ceramics inside. She had seen one of Frank's vases at a craft show, made enquiries about its maker, and discovered that he was somewhat local. After inviting Frank Hall to view her galleries, she commissioned a work as a present to herself for her sixtieth birthday.

Many vessels fell on his wheel before this beauty could rise, more delicate than his usual weightier stoneware, but still wide and generous in proportion. It had a lustered serpent chasing around the rim, over a body burnished with oxidized rings of hot gold. The day he presented the vase as complete, Catherine thought she had never seen such a radiant and cosmic glaze, nor her father so proud.

Her mother denied having touched it. She claimed that when she'd walked in, she'd found it already smashed on the stand.

Don't come near my studio.

Tell her about your girlfriend's money.

Stupid woman. I would pay to do what I do.

You do pay.

A replacement was made, but it lacked the planetary curves of the original; the new version had the look of a lesser reproduction. Her father still received generous payment for the commission—Catherine discovered later when he made a gift of a startling £25,000 to each of her children—but there was no compensation for the creative frustration that dogged him beyond the incident. With every failed attempt to reacquaint craft with inspiration, the pile of rejects burgeoned in the yard. Catherine reckoned these objects had been abandoned with good reason, as they were eerily deformed. When she said as much, asking her father to move the dump somewhere else, he barked, "Get used to it, young lady. It's permanent. I wouldn't think of moving it any more than I'd try and move Pompeii." Seeing his daughter's bewilderment, he told her to look up Vesuvius in the *Encyclopedia Britannica*, which she did to no immediate understanding. It was many years before she could wrap her mind around the analogy and figure out who was the victim and who was the volcano, and determine that her parents were a confusing mix of both. Gradually time and the elements worked a metamorphosis on the heap, with mold and leaves unifying the wreckage into one great hopeless masterwork that seemed to cry out with the burden of defeat.

With her father's anger subsiding into disappointment, grave enough to cast a pall over the household, the absence of any further denial of the breakage acted as confirmation of his wife's guilt.

Whether she had been given cause for provocation was less certain.

That the relationship between artist and patron had made her insanely jealous was clear, but whether she had been given grounds for suspicion was harder to establish. It never occurred to Catherine to ask—that would have been indelicate and to breach a boundary containing things too personal to discuss. After the incident, Catherine was taken to Rother Park by her father, and was finally introduced to infamous Kitty. Instead of meeting a femme fatale, she discovered an old lady in coral linen with platinum hair, and only a faint glimmer of glamour. She had greeted Catherine's father in a vague but friendly manner— he'd still managed to look dusty even though he'd washed and changed before going out. Catherine was sorry that Mrs. Lisle hadn't paid her more attention and recognized her specialness, but instead wasted time talking to everyone else who happened to be in the garden. In terms of revealing the lovers' complicity, the meeting was inconclusive. However, because her father had been paid well over the odds by Mrs. Lisle—*tell her about your girlfriend's money*—she could see how easily that could be construed as a sign of a special relationship, and fed into Catherine's mother's jealousy, justified or irrational. A likely scenario was that without the tools to temper a coiling tension, she became so tightly wound that she snapped.

Her mother broke things.

In another household it might have been a saucer or coffee mug, in hers it was trust and an Olmec and Etruscan–influenced bell krater.

She snapped because you can.

After the incident, her father made his own deliveries, and once a Mr. Durlacher, at the request of Mrs. Lisle, came to the farm to pick up a cardboard box. Catherine never saw or wondered what was inside—by then the eruptions of puberty were more compelling than her parents' intrigues. With her mother retreating behind a carapace of unhappiness, Catherine's prayers that she might get away from her eccentric parents and their shambolic farm were miraculously heard when she was told that she was going to board full-time at a school near Cranbrook. She never asked how the fees would be paid; that might have been to discover that a mistake had been made and there was no money for her to go. Applying a similar instinct to that of the school fees, Catherine never brought up the subject of the vase—avoiding questions was the best way of avoiding unpalatable answers, she quickly learned. Catherine received different explanations of her mother's passing when she drowned on her fifty-fifth birthday swimming in calm seas at Camber Sands, ranging from *Your mother did it to fuck us up* (her father) to *Poor Rosy's heart must have given out* (Catherine's maternal aunt). Catherine was at university when she heard the news. She returned home to find her father drunk, alternating grief with anger. He railed against his dead wife and claimed that her death had been a hostile act. "She baked me a cake, and left it on the table with tea. No note, Cath. She couldn't bring me down in life, so she'd bring me down with death."

Catherine was too stunned to know what to believe. In the absence of any psychiatric or medical evidence, the coroner ruled her mother's death an accident. With the person she would normally look to for answers gone, she was left hollow and weightless, as if her core had been ripped out and her center of gravity missing. She no longer recognized herself or her father. With her mother's act, they became strangers to each other, unreliable witnesses for having no clue or knowledge of what had been going on. In search of a place that would still be familiar, Catherine went back to university directly after the funeral. She didn't want to be around her father and listen to his drunken spewings. To stop and mourn the opaque woman who had been her mother would have been to comprehend and absorb something of her pain. The best she could do was launch back into her studies and finish her dissertation, and hope that whatever had happened, her mother hadn't suffered at the end.

With Rowan gone, and from the recesses of a darkened room, Catherine had a better understanding of what it was like to have been her mother. Like a caring companion, her own frailty had brought with it a more keenly developed compassion for her mother as she tried to fathom the anguish that had driven her to take her life. What had been her mental state before she died? Was she aware that she was suicidal? If she was, had she deliberately concealed her intentions? Now that she was five years away from the age that her mother had been when she died, Catherine saw similarities in herself but mostly differences. Whereas Catherine had sought solitude as a solace, her mother's isolation had been different. It hadn't been a choice for her: loneliness had only brought her despair.

There were other distinctions.

Unlike her mother, she was making an effort in case Rowan came home. She was doing it alone because she didn't want the help of bereavement counselors. She had consulted them about Rowan and they had failed to recognize her son's vulnerability. In doing so they had misadvised and betrayed her.

The morning of the accident they left the hospital and returned home. As it was still early, there was nothing for them to do except wait for Rowan to wake; they hadn't wanted to disturb him before and interrupt his last innocent sleep. At six thirty a.m., they heard stirrings in his room and had gone in to find him sitting at his computer. When he looked up, his placid eyes were already knowing. Catherine had managed to stop crying, but only for a moment. Rowan allowed her to hang rag-doll limp in his arms while she'd blurted out the news, accepting the information without any reaction. Michael later said that he was proud of his son's presence of mind and consoling strength; also, that he'd seemed to know his limits because when it was time, he'd walked them out of the room and closed the door behind them. Thirty minutes later Rowan was downstairs in his uniform, ready for school, refusing entreaties to stay home or be driven. He'd insisted on taking the bus as usual, and left the house with his earbuds in, just as if it were any ordinary day. A call to the headmaster confirmed that he was indeed there and was, to all outward appearances, fine.

On the way to the funeral, Rowan announced that he wanted to read at the service. The stoicism of this request had taken both parents by surprise.

After the priest intoned the service, Michael read Psalm 23, and "Amazing Grace" was sung, Rachel's school friend Charlotte Nestor took her turn to go to the lectern to speak. She told the congregation that Rachel had standards before any of her group knew what that meant, that she had an annoying tendency to always be right—but this made her the best person to turn to for advice. In opposing teams for debate, Rachel had taken her aside and said, *If I win, it's not personal*, which made being thrashed in front of the whole school seem all right. She spoke of her loyalty. "When Mum was ill, she came with me to the hospital. When Mum died, I remember Rache saying, *That's bloody awful*, and bursting into tears." Charlotte looked to the heavens, mugging slightly. "Sorry, Lord, for saying 'bloody.' Oh my God, that's twice! . . . Her last Facebook status was *Life=insane+beauty*. She was right. The beauty is that she existed. The insanity—the bloody awful part—is that she's gone." Her voice cracked. "I'm just so grateful to have known her."

The younger contingent burst into applause. Catherine saw that many of them were sobbing. She was moved by poor Charlotte and remembered the shock waves Sue Nestor's cancer had sent through her own family. She would never forget Jack Nestor's broken appearance at his wife's funeral and her own embarrassment in the face of his loss, at being helpless to do anything to relieve his suffering. She'd seen the same pitying looks and shame on faces when she'd entered the church, as if she had a terminal disease that was public knowledge but there was nothing more that could be done. No cure for being tired after driving from the country, having been out late at a party for a Chinese photographer in London the night before, because the Asian market was the fastest-growing area of contemporary art, and at the time that seemed so terribly important. No remedy for not following her instinct to say no to her daughter, and saying yes because it was so much easier than arguing the point. No absolution for being permissive when it suited her and strict when it did not, and for being the type of mother who passes for competent but is in truth neglectful.

Charlotte's bovine face was flushed with the effort of public speaking. She was trying so hard to honor her friend that she had the quality of an actress who had just nailed a part and was giving it her all. Although there was a lot of childish "I" in her speech, there was a brightness to her description that Catherine envied, making her question whether her own memories were already starting to fade. She asked herself what kind of mother she had been, taking Rachel to ballet before she could walk. To gymnastics before she could run. She remembered the fatigue of being with a tired and hungry child after school, and that when Rachel had become serious about tennis—and Rowan, for a while—she had made the au pair do the driving. Catherine helped with projects on the weekend, but only if they interested her; most often she was in the gallery, or racing up to see John Bramley in Norfolk. Rachel hadn't told her about Merhan or any other boyfriends—for all she knew there might have been many. She had once asked whether there was anyone she liked but had been met with a scathing gaze. *As if I would tell you.* The images of Rachel were blurred, but she realized that it wasn't her memory that was at fault, it was because during Rachel's short life she hadn't been present enough to see.

Then Rowan took his turn, walking up to the altar.

The sight of him by his sister's coffin was a double affront.

Someone had propped a tennis racket there. Rachel had been a talented player, one of the select few selected to participate in the "Way to Wimbledon" program sponsored by the club, requiring long hours of training, seven days a week, to the sacrifice of all her other extracurricular activities. She saw her own hubris that she had harbored so many hopes and ambitions for her daughter when all along this had been her destiny. Such efforts seemed wasteful now, and she wondered whether she should have encouraged her to spend more time at home or with friends relaxing, instead of putting her on a relentless treadmill. Perhaps the pressure had made her reckless? Literally, driven her to make foolish choices? She wanted to take the racket and smash it over the altar. Smash the false hope of resurrection. Cry and show God what punishment really meant.

But that wouldn't have been appropriate.

"I wrote this poem," Rowan said.

There was a collective holding of breath. Everyone was still in anticipation, except Michael, who squeezed her hand.

"That was the title," Rowan continued deadpan.

Everyone laughed, grateful at the release of tension, although

Catherine wasn't sure that this had been Rowan's intention. He didn't smile.

He continued at a measured pace.

Sixteen years pass
Is there a better way
or are we still the same?

Then, without making eye contact with anyone, Rowan walked back to his seat.

In contrast to the emotional release after Charlotte's speech, the congregation was nonplussed and silent. Then there was a polite rustle of movement, a fidgeting of programs and murmur, as if people felt obliged to react because to remain quiet might have seemed hostile or rude. Michael leaned in and whispered encouragingly, *Not bad. Almost a haiku.* Catherine could have kicked him for being so naïve. She thought that if Rowan was going to bother getting up there, he could have at least have found something nice to say about his sister. *Is there a better way* seemed to imply criticism of her—maybe of them all? Michael's interpretation of the poem was different. He thought his son's words were about as philosophical and inspirational as you could expect a fifteen-year-old boy's to be.

The day after the funeral, Rowan made another announcement. He informed his parents that he "wanted out of London" and to go away to school. In the context of his odd, affectless behavior—that he had yet to show one iota of sadness—his sudden declaration was alarming and seemed another way for Rowan to repress his feelings and run from his grief. Catherine took the news the hardest. The idea that Rowan would go away from home at a time of crisis, to a strange situation where he might not be supported, seemed a terrible one, and Catherine strenuously resisted the notion.

But Rowan insisted on going. He even made arrangements for himself, applying to a coed school outside Canterbury, where he was offered a provisional place, subject to parental consent. In the face of such determination, Catherine and Michael reluctantly agreed to consult three therapists and abide by majority rule. *Best of three* opinions, they said, believing no sane person would fail to take their side. After two meetings, they were overruled. The consensus was that as long as Rowan stayed in therapy, it was all right for him to go. His desire to leave was a way of taking charge of his emotions at a time of helplessness. The need to carve out an identity beyond the arena of mourning was positive—*basic survival*, one of them had said. Catherine was forced to submit. She didn't want to be accused of selfishly keeping him at home or using him as a crutch, but she believed that these experts had seriously underestimated the benefits of keeping the family together and was surprised by their failure to see what this meant. Two years before, when she had told Paige about plans for Hamdean, her friend had asked, "Are you sure? The rural idyll sounds all very lovely for small children, but now they are dreadful teenagers don't you want to stay in London, where you can get them out of your hair? You'll go mad in the country and the children won't want to come."

Catherine had dismissed her as being negatively disposed; possibly jealous of the fullness of her life, but it was ironic to think that in many ways, for different reasons, Paige had been right.

Shutting her laptop, she shuffled out through the back door to the garden. She had to remind herself to lift her chest and feet and walk properly. It was hard to believe that she had been athletic once: Center position netball, team undefeated. Then Pilates twice a week. Where had she found the energy or time?

Open post, check your email, walk a little.

All the days.

Crossing the grass, she followed the property line, keeping her gaze averted from the parcel of putting green of the sportsmen's lodge, absurdly manicured against the wild meadows on either side. The day was overcast, with only a few squibs of sunlight filtering through. Even so, she saw how the rays warmed the hawthorns for a moment before the cloud drifted into the light. She could see how tenderly the leaves were budding. They were vibrant, keen youngsters clambering over a hoary grandmother. Her heart ached again. She never used to look at nature this way, only if it was in a picture or representation, in a Ruisdael or Constable. This was another cruel irony of loss, that she could be half a person and the part that remained could become so much more acute.

Her thoughts were interrupted by the red car and its misplaced passenger.

She turned away and then turned back as she decided to retreat the most direct way inside, by crossing the grass to the front door. This had once been the original entrance, with recessed Ionian pillars and a pelmet weighted with a woven mass of wisteria on the surround. She noticed the wisteria too was budding, but the stems were smooth and lithe. On their first visit after exchanging contracts with the seller for Hamdean, Michael had warned her not to get too attached to the lovely blossoms: they were invasive and compromising the brickwork and fenestrations, and destined for the chop. The children had been with them at the time. Always alert to Michael's uncool general fogeyness, they'd howled with laughter and teased him all the way on the drive back to London. "Dad, would you open the *fenestration*, please?" "Did you know, Dad, that the eyes are the fenestrations of the soul?" Michael didn't mind being the butt of the joke as long as no one was being unkind. "Glad you lot are so easy to please," he'd said gamely. He couldn't resist a historical reference to justify his choice of vocabulary, with a digression into the seventeenth-century religious struggles in Bohemia and the Second Defenestration of Prague, where Protestants hurled a scribe and two Catholic Regents from a tower, and thus precipitated the Thirty Years' War. Rachel's takeaway from the lecture was delight in the verb *defenestrate*. "I can't believe there's such a buff and excellent word for throwing someone out of the window." Her reaction irked Rowan, who told his sister to stop using trendy expressions. What did "buff" mean? What was she trying to say? The discussion became semantic, with Catherine weighing in that buff was a neutral color and something you did to your car and nails. Her husband agreed that it was a kind of polishing, but could be stretched to mean a shining example— so her use wasn't totally out of line. Rachel was quick to crow to her brother, "Completely appropriate—see?" with Rowan deadpanning, *"That's cut. I'm blown,"* more Rachelisms, triggering another round of debate. Catherine missed their banter, the sustaining humor that balanced their frustrations and kept them all in check. Her children had given her much in the way of equilibrium. She wished she could say that she had done the same for them.

When Michael had sentenced the wisteria, Catherine had wholeheartedly agreed. She was as pragmatic as her husband; to be sentimental about a plant that would eventually undermine would have been bloody stupid. Looking again at the vines, two on the right, winding across to greet a smaller one on the left, she saw them as determined graces, more vigorous and alive, and worthy of a reprieve, than the staunchly inanimate façade that was little more than a shell. She decided to tell Michael that he should lay off the wisteria.

A girl's voice close by.

"Sorry to bother. I used to live here."

He was pleased, if a little surprised, to hear Catherine sounding so animated when she called to tell him about the girl. She said the girl had appeared on her doorstep, on her way somewhere else. She had decided spontaneously to stop by to see the place of her youth—Catherine reported this ironically, as the girl was eighteen and had just left school. She said that the girl was Clive Martin's daughter and had lived at Hamdean in the '90s when her mother, a French dancer, *whatshername*, had brought her over from Toulouse to play happy families and give her one-night romance with the director one more go. That ambition proved a folly and the relationship ended unhappily with the dancer going back to Paris to flit around and send her daughter away again, this time to stay with an aunt in Lyons—the poor thing had already been passed between various relatives. The child's name was Keira, although for a while Catherine seemed to prefer calling her *the girl*. Catherine said she was sparky and had an unusual quality. "You would have been fascinated by her. Other than you, she's the only person in the world who cares where the boiler room used to be. That's why the living room has that high slip of a window—it was the only light source for the original boiler room! You always said that the French doors were an anomaly and that the developers must have been in league with the planners to allow them to be put in. Well, you were right if there was no pre-existing opening. She couldn't get over the transformation—said it used to be a total dungeon in there. . . . Do you know that there used to be a maze of box hedges on the terrace? She said they were 'scrawny but good for finding robins' nests.' I felt sorry for her. She's obviously had a difficult time, treated like an accessory, pulled out when needed, thrown away when not. You have to wonder how broke and desperate her mother must have been to uproot an eight-year-old to live with someone you've only met once—even if he is the father of your child. Let's face it, the life-span of a dancer is about the same as a moth. She's taking a gap year and doing temp jobs when she can."

By the time they had finished talking, Michael had Googled the director Clive Martin. He read that he did have a daughter by the ballet dancer Marine Deveaux. Her name was Keira Martin, as Catherine had said. He had already heard about the director. When he and Catherine were negotiating for the house, the estate agent had put in a one-sheet about Clive Martin along with the specs. He'd thought it savvy, the use of glamorous forebears in the advertising: mystique and provenance were all part of a package for which people paid good money.

The next day, Catherine went to London. They met each other for dinner that evening, tentatively holding hands as they walked along the New Kings Road. They stopped at a new tapas restaurant that was dimly lit and cozy and run by noisy Andalusians; they avoided going anywhere they had ever been with the children. Over a plate of oily pulpo, she told him that all was seemingly functioning at the gallery, but admitted that it was time for her to step up during the selection for the group show. She needed to do the rounds, make sure the best work was going in, otherwise she would be negligent. She was building up to see a Northern Irish artist she represented, Aggie Mackay, who built layers of lacquered newspaper in floorscapes, or *Soul-maps*, as they were called. All a good sign. When she left to go to the bathroom between courses, Michael looked in her Boots shopping bag and saw that she had refilled the antidepressants prescribed to her by her GP—not a bad thing as well. She'd said that she couldn't tell whether the medication had made any difference but was giving it the benefit of the doubt. Michael couldn't see much change in her, apart from sleeping more than usual. Whilst it was good that she was rested, it was also bad for any hope of sex.

As she undressed for bed and leaned down to pull off her shoes, he saw the slope of her back. She'd always had beauti-ful shoulders, imbued and sculpted by an athleticism that went with her determined, head-of-hockey sexiness he had always found so attractive. Her muscles were denuded now; the ridges of her vertebrae formed a distinct bony crest. No longer a radi-ant host of pheromones, her skin had sallowed and stretched tightly across her spine. There was pathos in her alteration, yet awe that her body could still make him stir after twenty-seven years. Desire didn't flare in the way that it used to do, but then nothing could match the volatile lust of the early days, when they would meet in the studio that she shared with a friend and squeeze into the bathroom in case of her roommate's return. How determinedly she guarded against interruption, locking themselves inside the tiny space, where they stripped each other, crouched and sucked, getting some knocks and bruises from the sink—the urgency of their needs had been a pleasurable surprise to them both. Sex continued to be robust, with a natural tapering after marriage and with another dip in frequency after the children were born. It was understandable that Catherine had become unreachable in the last year, but that didn't stop him wanting her or remembering how it used to be between them. He saw her lift off her bra, quickly smother her body in an outsize nightshirt, and give him a rueful glance that told him sorry, whatever he was wanting she wouldn't be able to give him tonight—or, as he interpreted, anytime in the foreseeable future. He watched her slide between the sheets and roll away onto her side, with her back looking as approachable and welcoming as a face of Mont Blanc. His vital signs pulsed, *I'm still here.* He would have liked to make love to her to shake off his sadness, but the moment quickly passed as he heard her breathing slow with her descent into sleep.

When they had spoken on the phone the day before, after establishing that neither one had heard from Rowan, he'd asked, "Do you think she'll ever return?"

She had understood that he was talking about Keira. "I invited her back, actually. Whether she'll come, who knows?"

Michael was glad to hear of her offer, as he'd become curious about Keira as well.

One of his last thoughts before drifting into slumber that night was a hope that he might meet her. He had questions about some foundations he'd found in the garden; whether during her time there had been some type of structure—a summerhouse, perhaps? In the morning, he would ask Catherine whether Keira had mentioned one.

He also hoped that Catherine hadn't scared her away.

The first weekend it was warm and sunny: everyone spilled out to the courtyard, lying on the grass and steps to take advantage of the heat. Like most of the school, the quad had been built in the '30s and nodded back to traditional forms while looking forward to modernism. With white-boxed windows and spare stucco lines, the overall effect was attractive in a utilitarian way. Most of the students were already in groups, but Rowan felt no pressure to join them. After being the target of so much attention at home, being anonymous was a relief and it was liberating to walk around unnoticed—a bit like being invisible in a stealth game, moving about under the radar, evading an unspecified enemy. He was aware that he should make the most of this new advantage, as he knew it wouldn't last.

Canterbury Downs had a good vibe—a bonus, as he'd chosen it randomly from the Internet. Rowan had scanned the school's website, clocked its off-center, arty philosophy, and seen that it had no uniform and offered A-level courses he liked.

It was a plus that he'd had to go really low on the page to find anything about phys ed.; a novelty that there was a lot of talk about *emotional development* and *balance*. The laid-back atmosphere of the students seemed to testify to this experience.

He'd met his neighbors in the house that morning Fred and Osei (or Oz, Ozzy, or Ozman as he was variously known). Fred had come from Holland Park Comp. He'd been sent away because his parents were under the illusion that he couldn't get drugs outside of London. Osei was the son of Ghanaian diplomats, a hyperactive math wiz and electronic-sound geek who never stopped moving, dodging punches with an imaginary sparring partner. He had already been at the school two years. "If you don't mind greasy food and greasy girls, the place is all right," he told Rowan. "I eat healthily—like to take care of myself."

Fred objected, "You eat so much junk."

Osei pulled up his T-shirt to show a six-pack. "I supplement. I'm vegetarian. I have to because here in Great Britain, you call one hairy piece of lettuce a salad when it's garnish." Fred cracked up. Rowan figured this was an in-joke of sorts. Osei chuckled, tucking his T-shirt into his jeans, nodding toward his friend, "For him the only side-salad is grass." They admitted to being *mellow* and that they were going back out into the woods to get even more mellow—they told him the safest place to smoke *da garnish* was behind the pet shed, where the lonely kept rabbits and rats. Fred hoped the wind was blowing in the right direction, otherwise *them bunnies and rodents are getting high*. They invited Rowan to join, but he said, *Later.* Osei did some more air boxing, then with a tucking motion he and Fred were gone. Rowan was okay when they went. He'd never been one for partying, preferring clarity to stonersville. He wanted to go back to his room and think.

Lying on his bed, duvet and cover not yet united but comfortably entwined underneath, he had time to get his bearings, allowing himself to be pleased and quite a lot relieved that the compass directing him was working well enough to have got him so far. Being away in a new environment had made him feel a nice, newly mature calm, where he could acknowledge and respond to where he was at without being so fucking reactive all the time—for sure this wouldn't have been possible if he'd stayed at home. He could lie there and consider his situation without getting worked up, revisit episodes that had exasperated him before and see them in a different light, and be grateful that they had set him off and pushed him a few steps closer to where he was now.

His attitude toward the carnations was an example. His reaction to them before had been harsh. He'd found them on the steps of the front door—he'd already waded knee-deep through plastic bouquets on the path to get to them. The petals had been spray-painted electric blue and their stems gold the way people did pinecones at Christmas. The idea that someone would dye a flower and an even bigger twat pay money for a bunch, and leave it with a note: "Love you Rache. Missing you so much," or "RIP wherever you are, *will never forget Glastonbury*," had made him want to go as far away as possible from where anyone knew there was a Rachel. He despised the flowers. If his mother hadn't been waiting for him inside, he would have taken them and put them straight into the bin.

It wasn't just the lurid flowers that offended, it was the disrespect to her extinction to keep talking to her as if she were alive. The messages and bouquets were mawkish, and he couldn't stand the way his mum had lapped them up with a tragic thirst as if they could actually make her relationship with Rachel any less crap.

He'd seen the only way forward was to move on.

This didn't mean he didn't care. He'd overheard whispers that he was cold and unfeeling, which was rubbish because he cared more about Rachel than everyone put together. He'd gone with her in his mind, living her last moments being mangled in a car—imagining her pain, terror, disbelief, before she became nothing.

Wrapping his thoughts around the elimination of her consciousness was its own massive head trip. He saw her brain as having been wiped like a hard drive, with millions of gigabytes gone—he pictured one final burst of activity this way as she had constantly been hooked up to the Internet. That done, he wasn't buying into the collective hysteria that cheapened emotion and wasn't changing a thing. His experience of her was exactly that: his own—he resented all the pressure to share, join revisionism, myth-making, and her elevation to a sainthood that distorted her into someone he didn't know. At the funeral, he had listened to Char Nestor turn a story about Rachel trying to spook her before a debate into one about kindness and friendship. In the same speech, she had made out that Rachel was so sympathetic when Char's mother had died, when really what Char had been describing was that Rachel had been selfish enough to co-opt her grief by managing to cry first. Ordinarily, he wouldn't have paid much attention to what Rachel or Char Nestor said, but now Rachel was dead, he was more inflexibly attached to what had been, even if it wasn't flattering. As he explained in a session with his new school's impressively impassive therapist, who operated on Fridays in a tidy cubicle off the sick bay, he used to get on better with her, but she'd changed. She'd become mercenary.

The therapist, whose name was Lakme, asked, "What do you mean?"

"Mercenary—as in, you only care about money."

"I meant, in what way?" she qualified with persistent calm. She wasn't easily ruffled. Lakme was in her forties—even her olive skin refused to wrinkle.

"She wanted to be rich. That was her ambition. Her goal."

He saw Lakme's stare intensify, a pulling of focus. He was satisfied that he had made her disapprove of Rachel too.

"Do you have one? A goal?"

"Of course," he'd said without saying what, because this wasn't entirely true.

Lakme didn't push him to reveal what. She was prioritizing. The directness of her next question surprised him.

"What was your last memory of your sister?"

Water, almost black. Silver reflection. Lights slashing the water like knives.

"She texted me a picture of her boyfriend's indoor swimming pool the day she died."

"She sent you a photograph?"

"Yeah. From her cell phone."

"Why do you think she wanted you to see that?"

"Advertising, I suppose."

"A swimming pool?" Her voice was level, he thought, to hide her incredulity.

He wondered why therapists did that; they pretended not to have opinions when obviously they did, otherwise they wouldn't be there. It was obvious what she wanted to know: what his sister was trying to prove by sending him that image. He could have said that she enjoyed provoking him, knowing that he didn't approve of her Eurotrash friends. She liked to tease him with accounts of obscene wealth—who had the biggest houses, the biggest cars. When he'd point out that the bigger the car, the bigger the polluter, she laughed and said, "Who cares? I like them. They're smooth." He didn't tell Ms. Lakme how she liked to embarrass him by calling him into her room when she was half-naked or when she was I-chatting with a friend who was also undressed, call him *prude* when he complained. Or that when she didn't get into the secondary school of choice after hours of private tutoring, she had a fit and everyone was shocked—except him. He knew she wouldn't get in; that was a no-brainer. She wasn't academic or particularly studious. When he asked his dad why he was so amazed—"She isn't exactly the sharpest pencil in the box,"—his father told him to stop being supercilious, adding, "Don't ever tell her that." Rowan tried to be sympathetic. He even gave up tennis and substituted running, a sport he didn't like, because every time he won a tournament and she didn't, she'd go into decline. Then she went to a suitably sloaney school, but somewhere in the transition she became hard—talk about supercilious! They got into the habit of sniping at each other—he was sure she started it. He didn't need a therapist to explain why: she was shallow, a bit thick, and she minded. She wanted to be something else. But he withheld all that, and more. He had to give Ms. Lakme somewhere to go in their sessions every week, otherwise they would get bored. Also, he was watching the clock on her desk—it had a wide face and stumpy legs—his first-period environmental studies class was about to start and he didn't want to be late. He'd met the teacher, Mr. Stewart, at orientation and he seemed all right. Instead, he responded, "She didn't know she was going to die."

Ms. Lakme scribbled something on her pad.

There was another reason that his sister's deification bothered him. It was totally missing the point of the message of her death: the urgency of life.

This and neon carnations he contemplated lying on his bed the first night he arrived. He was cautiously excited. He had the sense that something was going to happen. He was poised for something: not greatness exactly—he was too modest to have thought that—but verging.

He had the beginnings of a manifesto.

Do no harm.

(He knew that was a given.)

Live every day as if it mattered.

That was harder to do and as important.

He could hear manic fits of laughter next door. Osei and Freddie were yelling "Garnish the mushroom!" and crying with laughter. He heard a hollow thud that sounded like a head bumping against the wall.

Morons, he thought with a smile.

When Keira returned to Hamdean she wasn't in the red car. She came on foot, as she didn't drive—it turned out that when she'd visited before she had been given a lift to the house by a friend. When Catherine heard that Keira had walked three miles from the station, along narrow lanes with no footpath, where maniacs drove blind corners as if they owned the roads, she was appalled and told her that if only she'd known she was arriving, she would have gladly met her train. Seeing her host's anxiety, Keira reminded her that as she'd never taken her email or number, short of communicating by snail-mail or carrier pigeon, without days of notice it might have been hard to arrange, making them both smile at the notion.

Since her last visit the young woman had smartened up. With her hair combed down, blazer cinched at the waist, canvas weekend bag in hand, she looked more like a chic French student from a Boden catalogue than the arty punk she'd met several weeks before. Safety concerns aside, Catherine wasn't fazed by her arrival, as her invitation had been sufficiently welcoming and open-ended to warrant a certain flexibility— although she wouldn't have said no to the chance to organize herself: get food, check the guest bedroom, make sure there was toilet paper in the spare bathroom, and so on, but her lack of preparation didn't diminish her cautious excitement at the young woman's return.

As there was nothing in the fridge, Catherine had to improvise supper. There was a small roast in the freezer but no time to let it thaw. She overestimated the defrost setting on the microwave. This probably accounted for the unappetizing gray hue of the beef. Not that Keira seemed to mind. Using her fork to saw her meat, she managed to put away a fair amount for someone with such a slight frame. While she was eating, Catherine plied her with questions. She wanted to draw her out, hear more of her story. She was moved by this waif with flickering eyes and acne-picked skin who had never known a family.

After leaving school, Keira had made the conscious decision not to go to university. She hadn't seen the point of trying. Since the financial meltdown there were no jobs, even for those with qualifications. She seemed to think that this had leveled the playing field. She had come back to the UK from France to go to sixth-form college and live with a host family in Reading. Her aunt had subsidized her rentrée on the understanding that once exams were done there wouldn't be further financial help. As Keira's father died of a stroke at the age of sixty-five (he'd been much older than his wife), and her mother a couple of years after, she had no immediate family left in the UK—not that she'd really known them or they had been much help. She told Catherine that she was glad to be getting a head start in the work arena while everyone else was loading their résumés with extra degrees, calling her decision "betting on myself." Catherine listened sympathetically. Her argument showed drive, yet she could see the logic behind it was flawed. She was conscious that if either one of her children had tried to shelter behind such a naïve idea, she would have been obliged to point out the cold reality that fewer jobs meant stiffer competition; in the present economy, it was all the more important to get as many qualifications as possible, but she didn't say anything as it was too late: Keira's decision had already been made.

Keira was temping through an agency. So far this meant a revolving door of offices, replacing sick receptionists, and doing basic secretarial work, but she was confident that sooner or later she'd get the entrée she desired.

"Where would that be?" Catherine asked.

"In design or fashion—I'd kill for a job on a magazine," she said.

Although her description was sufficiently vague to cover a multitude of options, Catherine immediately thought of Paige, who was in the best position to advise. She offered to text her in the morning. She would put them in touch; they could talk and, maybe, *you never know*, Paige might be of help. The suggestion seemed to thrill Keira. Connecting with the editor of *Charisma* she said would be *major*. She went as far as to declare the magazine "the best of the *middle-aged glossies.*" Seeing Catherine's amusement, she quickly added, "Obviously, I wouldn't say that to her face."

After dinner Catherine told her about Rachel.

Keira paused for a moment, then said: "I knew there was something about you."

Catherine was grateful for her lack of commentary. There was nothing for her to add.

Catherine also spoke about Rowan. "Losing his sister was harder on him than anyone. I'm understanding more now, why he needed to get away."

At the mention of his name, Keira got up from the table and moved toward the dresser, where ceramics, postcards, and photographs were displayed on a shelf. Keira peered at an image of Rowan and Rachel taken at a tennis tournament when they were aged eleven and twelve. They had been away at sports camp for several weeks that summer. Prolonged exposure to the sun had turned their skin gold.

"He looks a lot different—he's sixteen now," Catherine added. "You can't imagine a sweeter boy. Even when he was small, he'd ask questions: *If ants were bigger would people still want to squash them?* He's perfect, except he doesn't want to be around me anymore."

The day of the tournament they had both placed in their categories. Rowan was always modest about his achievements—he had won several times before. *It's only a game,* his expression in the photograph seemed to say. It was Rachel's first win after several years of competing, and she enjoyed every moment of it.

She held up her racket by the paddle in both hands, in imitation of a Wimbledon Cup winner's triumphal clinch.

"Rachel cared more than she let on. She laughed anything that bothered her away."

"I get that," Keira said. She turned from the photograph and dropped into a seat at the far end of the table, where Catherine's laptop was lying open. "Rowan sounds cool. I'll Facebook him." She began to type with relish.

Her sudden interest in Rowan was disconcerting. As much as Catherine was enjoying their friendship, it was premature for her to be making an independent connection with her son. Before she could demur, Keira had logged on.

"Hm . . ." She peered at the screen. "Not the only Rowan Hall on Facebook. This one might be doing time. And this one is . . . a retired engineer." She frowned, still tapping away at the keyboard. "Are you sure he has an account?"

"Of course I'm sure." Catherine checked herself, knowing that resistance would be unattractive. She tried to compensate, "Actually I don't know, as I'm banned from friendship on grounds of my age. He says that Facebook is only for the young. *'Trust me I won't be doing this when I'm twenty-five.'*"

"Wise child," Keira said distractedly, still searching.

Yes, he is, Catherine thought, but didn't say.

Soon Keira was defeated, slumping down at the table. "If he was on, he's not anymore."

Catherine made no further effort to disagree.

"Maybe I'll meet him, one of these days. "

"You would like each other," Catherine felt obliged to say.

Later, in the privacy of her room, she texted Rowan: "What's happening with your Facebook account?" At one thirty a.m. he replied: "Cancelled. Total waste of time." She made a mental note not to share his response with Keira. She didn't want to say anything more to encourage her pursuit.

They went to bed just after midnight and passed through the hall. This was Michael's favorite part of the house, as it still had many of its original features: foliated fireplace, acanthus moldings, and stained oak paneling. He had bought a Regency drum table for the center, which he placed over a precious Isfahan rug that had been a gift to Catherine from the artist John Bramley. Behind the table was the oil sketch of Sutton Hoo that she'd seen on her first studio visit; the lilting rhomboids that she had perceived as vessels to be filled and floated—with her understanding of their destination to come beside the grave. On her departure the next day, he had given her the picture, wrapped in newspaper—an extraordinary generosity, all the more amazing as he had recognized her connection with the image when she had seen it only briefly. She accepted the gift; to refuse would have been churlish, foolish if she were viewing it in artistic or monetary terms; besides, she wanted the painting and appreciated the spirit in which it had been given. She had to consider the ethics of taking it off the market from Katz, but quickly waived the issue, calculating that this was a private gesture between her and John Bramley of greater importance than any commission, as it presaged their future together; the truth of this was borne out by their long collaboration, intimacy, and friendship. Their relationship wasn't sexual, nor was it sexless. Occasionally she allowed herself to become something other, when he would politely say, *May I look at you?* and she undressed for him, allowing him to cast his eyes over her body with a gaze that was clinical, like a physician looking over a patient or anatomical model. She enjoyed those moments, as she could escape being Catherine, become flesh for him and forget who she was. There was also a sublimated pleasure in knowing that his interest was not just academic; for all his interest in the human form, he admired and desired her too. After these interludes, before the conversation could return to the order of the day, there was always an adjustment period while Catherine put on her clothes, fastened her blouse. His eyes became liquid as if he were dematerializing her image, dissolving and internalizing it to make it his own. His final look was always sorrow. Sometimes, she understood this to be sadness for the passing of time, the remorselessness of experience that made every second the obsolescence of the one before. In other moments, she saw his sadness was the mirror of her own: his eyes were the reflection of hers. These explorations ended with his failing health, but she remained steadfastly his representative and caretaker. The painting of Sutton Hoo and, later, a fine Isfahan rug were unapologetically hers to possess. Just as he had always occupied her mind, the painting and the rug had furnished her house, representing the life they might have had together, the one he had offered her but that she had declined.

Keira stopped in front of the picture and stared at it with an intensity that made Catherine hold her breath. Then she looked toward the stairs. "In this direction nothing's changed." With that quick shift of attention, Catherine detected a French accent in her four-syllable pronunciation of *direction*. Before that she had only spoken perfect estuary English.

Her new focus of interest was the wooden paneled staircase. It had been hung with murky Jacobean ancestral portraits, purchased in a half-dozen lot at Christies South Ken. These dark, padded dandies rose up incongruously to a portrait of Michael's father that was painted on his retirement. He stared out wearily from the frame in a plain gray suit.

She looked down at the flagstones, "Or here. We walked all over this floor without noticing it, yet here it still is, the same. Incredible. . . . But when I look there"—she stared at the wall at the end of the hall where their apartment ended and the partition began—"it's weird. There was a green baize door in the paneling." She moved toward the area. "All gone."

"That would have been torn out when the developers did the conversion," Catherine rued. "I don't know why this building wasn't listed."

Keira didn't seem to hear. "A maze of corridors. Everything smaller. Rooms, windows, low ceilings, old kitchen with an iron range." She turned to Catherine, eyes bright with intent. "We could get a hammer, see if it's still there."

Catherine laughed. "I never knew how it was before, so I don't have the same . . ." She joined her at the wall. "But now you mention it . . ." She slapped the partition and heard a hollow thud. The construction was low-quality and had been done on the cheap. Even so, her palms stung at the affront. She hit the panels again: another empty thud. "My neighbor must be wondering . . ."

"Who?" Keira said innocently, before giggling with mischief. As a parting gesture, she thumped the wall as well.

As they went upstairs, Keira rapped the panels with her knuckles. "I'd do this every night. I was convinced there was a secret passage. I thought a door would spring open if I could find it."

"You sound as though you were trying to escape."

"Yeah." She shrugged wryly. "Be careful for what you wish for, right? They sent me to live in bloody France and they knew I didn't want to go."

Her lack of self-pity was impressive and demonstrated strength of character. Yet, behind all her bravado, Catherine could see the effort it was taking for her to resist becoming the victim of her story. She'd been cast out once, but she was refusing to be reeled back in.

"They thought going away would benefit you, surely?"

"I don't think anyone noticed I'd left. There were always so many people around. Here one day, gone the next."

"That must have been difficult."

Keira nodded solemnly. "When you are as rich and semi-famous as my father was, you always have somebody to play with and you always have guests."

The way she said "guests" made them sound like locusts or pests.

She pursed her lips, indicating that was all she wanted to say.

Catherine would have liked to ask more about this strange

circus of a household, complete with vanishing players and infestations, but didn't probe further. She wanted to respect Keira's privacy much as she had hers when she'd spoken about Rachel. Catherine credited Keira's survival to her brave attitude and reckoned there was much to be learned from this young person.

At the top of the first landing, Catherine led her visitor along the corridor to the guest suite—she never considered putting her in one of the children's rooms. Brief as their occupancy had been, the top floor would always be Rachel and Rowan's domain.

Seeing the spare bedroom again, Catherine was pleasantly reminded of its elegance and charm. The room had been kitted out to a higher standard than any other in the house, with pale-blue damask draping the length of the tall windows, linens of an even higher thread count than she had on her own bed—but never used. Finally, here was someone to enjoy all its comforts. Keira nodded and began to unpack. She threw down her jacket, where it splayed over the low upholstered chair, and pulled out a sponge bag from her hold-all, leaving Catherine to hover at the door, waiting for words of approval or thanks that didn't come. Instead, they said good night. Only later, when she was about to fall asleep, did she realize that this had been as satisfying as any words of gratitude. Being taken for granted was underrated; it was, perhaps, one of the greatest luxuries of all.

Catherine had set her alarm for six a.m. with the idea of getting up before Keira to prepare breakfast, as she had said she wanted to leave early. In the morning, when she went downstairs, she was surprised to find her young guest already up and sitting at her laptop in the kitchen.

"Hope you don't mind," she said, nodding at the pot of tea and half-eaten toast. "I woke up starving." She indicated the computer by way of explanation. "Was just looking up train times."

"That's quite all right," Catherine reassured, although at that time in the morning, her ease and presumption was less attractive than it had seemed the night before.

They exchanged telephone numbers after breakfast. As promised, Catherine texted Paige about Keira. *Have a young friend interested in fashion. Would you pls meet her for advice?* To Paige's credit, she was quick to respond: *Have her come to the office midday Monday week. After that I'm gone to Milan & NYC.*

"I'm there!" Keira whooped when Catherine showed her Paige's reply.

Catherine texted back *many thanx*, along with Keira's phone number. The meeting was set. Keira couldn't stop smiling as if she couldn't believe her luck.

Soon it was time for Keira's departure. After collecting her bag, she stopped in the hall, glancing around one last time. "Goodbye, house," she said with an air of finality.

"But you'll be back soon, won't you?" Catherine was emphatic. This was a statement, not a question.

Keira looked away. At first Catherine thought she had been too insistent and embarrassed her, but when the young woman faced her again she saw that her lips were trembling.

"I have wanted to come back here for so long to remind

myself that I was once here and that I . . . mattered." Her voice cracked as she struggled to find the words. "I had all these ideas about making peace with myself, and getting 'closure'—I know that sounds corny, but it was what I needed to do. Never in my wildest dreams did I imagine I would meet someone so genuinely kind and amazing as you."

Keira stepped forward and leaned her head on Catherine's chest. Startled by her sudden declaration, Catherine pulled her closer, wrapping her arms around the girl's small frame. She held her, savoring the contact, the girl's damp breath on her skin, the musky smell of patchouli in her hair. Hearing her say, "It's much nicer here now, it's a home," was strangely gratifying, even though the compliment had not been earned. She and Michael had taken possession of the house just over two years before; after that it had been under construction most of that year. Apart from two visits, and one weekend when work was almost done, they hadn't spent any time there with the children. Hamdean was never a family home—only an unrealized dream of one. Yet hearing it described as such gave Catherine satisfaction. As if by making an impression on the girl, she had accomplished something of importance.

t was brisk out, colder than Catherine had expected. The brightness of the morning had suggested a milder day. They were alone on the platform. The station was small and didn't service many: no ticket office, just a loading bay, a covered bench, and a footbridge over two tracks leading to a second platform with another covered bench. Beyond that a field of woodrush and buttercup was hung with mist, seemingly oblivious to the intrusions of the railway. Keira hugged her chest and side-stepped to keep warm. Catherine offered her scarf but Keira refused to take it. With a stubborn resilience typical of her age, she insisted that she was fine without.

Soon the train eased into the station. With only four carriages it was as compact as one of Rowan's old toys. Keira boarded the train and leaned out of the window while the conductor went up and down the platform checking doors. Catherine wished her best of luck for the interview. "When you meet Paige, be sure to—" She was about to give her some background information on Paige, how she needed to be handled, et cetera, but she noticed that Keira wasn't listening. She was looking at a man who had edged behind her to use the corridor for a loud conference on his mobile phone. The pinstripes on his regimented city suit made Catherine think of Michael and reminded her of his question. "I meant to ask, behind the old topiary, was there a gazebo or summerhouse?"

This seemed to get Keira's attention. The girl considered for a moment and pouted slightly; she did that when she was serious. "No. I don't remember anything there. Can't have been in my time." Her lips curved into a smile that Catherine was learning to recognize was effortful. "But then again, I wasn't at Hamdean very long."

The conductor waved his flag and sounded the whistle for departure.

With one last *Good luck with the interview* from Catherine, a *Will call you after* from Keira, the girl stepped back into the carriage and the train pulled away.

On return to the house Catherine went straight to the kitchen. She left the breakfast plates uncleared, as the casual messiness of cups and crumbs seemed to infuse life into the space. She allowed herself the satisfaction of thinking that the visit had been a success; by trusting each other and sharing their experiences they had grounded their friendship. For her own part, she was glad to have done something constructive for Keira by setting her up with Paige; the meeting had the potential of being a life-changing break. She only hoped that she was ready for opportunity and had been sufficiently prepped.

She had intended to say more to her at the station, but on the platform she had seemed distant and withdrawn. On reflection, the way she had refused her scarf, lifting her hand as if to say *stop* had been a signal to back off. She hadn't taken this personally, as a little introspection after an intense couple of days was perfectly understandable. She probably didn't need any more advice. *Stop worrying*, Catherine told herself. Keira would manage just fine.

She took out Rachel's mobile phone that she carried with her at all times. A social worker had returned it to her in London in a clear plastic bag, along with her daughter's other belongings: mascara, lip gloss, birth-control pills, Oyster Card, student ID, and a change purse containing five one-pound coins. Jackie, the original social worker, had not come. At the time Catherine had wondered whether her outburst at the hospital might have been the reason Jackie had sent a terrified-looking surrogate. The new social worker cradled a second parcel in her arms, double wrapped in opaque paper and plastic. Her hesitant manner and the presentation of the package told Catherine what it was.

"I have Rachel's bag." She swallowed. Like Jackie she was pale. Catherine wondered whether she ever saw the light of day. "I should warn you there are—"

"Thanks." Catherine took the parcel. She couldn't help being abrupt. It was agonizing to watch her tiptoe around the fact that it was stained. She didn't want reminding of the carnage that night. Nor was it conceivable that she would allow one of her daughter's belongings to be incinerated and treated as hazardous waste. After some deliberation, she put the parcel directly into a drawer in Rachel's bedroom cupboard. There was nothing to be gained by dwelling on her blood.

Her decision to put away Rachel's bag was made tolerable only by the possession of Rachel's mobile telephone; there was a purpose to having that and keeping it close. After guessing the PIN—1234—Catherine accessed a dizzying stream of conversations between Rachel and her friends, discussions of social plans written in a shorthand: *Bizzy ha . . . not going. Wtf? Wat about cruxy? . . . Shame, no. Tarnished!* She couldn't decode the meaning, nor did she try. She was more interested in her mood, which was lighthearted and suffused with her brand of irreverence and humor. The texts, which she read many times, only went back three weeks, as it was a replacement for one that had been lost. Rachel's carelessness with her technology had been a source of friction between them.

She studied Merhan's texts carefully. According to Rowan he had been Rachel's boyfriend of several weeks. There was one saved voicemail from him, apparently from shortly after they had met: "It was really good to see you. Um. I have been thinking about you a lot. When I say a lot, I mean *all the time.* Hope your foot is better." (Catherine wasn't aware of Rachel having any foot problems.) "Yeah, again, uh, it was good to see you. Bye."

After that they texted back and forth.

Can you stay? We will have stars for light and sunshine in the morning, he asked.

She responded by sending a photo of herself smoldering into the camera.

I want to I will try

They sent pictures to each other, demonstrating a variety of poses, from sultry doe eyes to frowns. Merhan appeared older than seventeen. With slick black hair and a humorous mouth, he was attractive. He was more like a man than a boy. In her photographs, Rachel looked soft and sensual, as if someone had taken an eraser to her precise nose and jaw and rubbed away any distinct edges.

I crave u, she wrote.

Merhan's affection for Rachel made it impossible for Catherine not to like this ardent man-boy. His voicemail and texts humanized him, diffusing her rage at him for being the driver of the car that had killed her daughter. Seeing his face was a reminder that she was not the only one to have lost a child, making her regret her behavior toward his parents all the more. She had harangued Mr. and Mrs. Azadi at the hospital for deviating from the plan, as if there had been one; she hadn't known herself what Rachel was doing that night. Realizing her wrong, she had written a letter of apology and hand delivered it to the Azadis' home. Even after it was returned by courier the same day, *Please—do not contact us again* printed across the envelope, she had still wanted to be near. A week later, after Rowan and Michael had gone to bed, she had driven to the Azadis' home in Kensington. She had parked opposite the double-fronted exterior and sat in her car watching the house. It was after midnight but the house was ablaze with light as people of all ages came and went. They huddled together and clutched one another. They grieved loudly, demonstratively; as it was with her, the difference between night and day no longer had meaning to this family. The second night of her vigil, a police cruiser had pulled up alongside Catherine's car. The police officer got out and asked Catherine what she was doing: a suspicious woman had been reported in the area. A complaint had been made. *Don't worry*, Catherine told the officer. *I won't be back.* True to her word she never returned. She didn't want to cause the family any further disturbance.

It was to the conversations between her own family members that she always returned. She had read them so many times that she knew all the words. The ones between Rachel and Rowan demonstrated a tender reliance that she hadn't known existed. They checked in with each other during the day, with Rachel most often initiating the conversation, although sometimes Rowan contacted her first. He told her about a 10K trial run and she teased him for running like a chicken. He texted her the day after having a "weird dream." She answered: *Dreams r boring—only interesting to yourself.* When Rowan went into details of the dream—he was in a tent with her, fighting, because she had installed central heating—she was delighted:

IM SO NAFF!

I know. We'd borrowed mum's rugs. The radiators were leaking oil. I was freaking out. It was traumatic

haha!

The evening before the accident Rowan had given her the heads up: *Dad is looking for you.*

I'm hanging here with Merhan, she replied.

Don't you have exams tomorrow? Revision? History of the Plebians?

Fuck off. Why don't you come with? Mira's here in a sexy bikini

When he didn't reply, Rachel sent her brother a photograph of herself in Mira's swimming pool.

Rowan wasn't the only family member to contact her that night. Up until then Michael's texts had been a mixture of amazing facts and educational bulletins. Three days before he had corresponded with Rachel about Amy, the largest rabbit in the world, a Continental Giant, complete with statistics and exclamations galore.

3 stone? A beast!! I want one!!! please?

Ask your mother, Michael replied. This was a refrain. Several days later he repeated these words. They were his last to Rachel.

The night before the accident Catherine had been out all evening at an art opening, followed by a long, boozy dinner with a collector who was in town for the sales. When Michael had returned home late from work and discovered that Rachel was still out, he texted to find her whereabouts.

Can I stay over with Mira? We r doing homework, was Rachel's answer. This was only a partial truth, as she had been at her house before leaving to go joyriding with Mira's brother, Merhan.

Ask your mother, he had written back, which Rachel dutifully did.

Catherine's own messages to her daughter had as much warmth as a bus schedule. *What time? Have you got . . . ? Did you do?* Yet when Rachel texted, *Can I stay over at Mira's tonight?* Catherine never replied, and Rachel had taken this to mean consent. It was eleven thirty p.m. when Catherine finally returned home and realized that Rachel was still out. She made the judgment that it was too late for her to come back—it was better for her to stay with her friend than make her travel at a late hour. *It's probably fine,* she had said to Michael. Several hours later, in the early hours of the morning, Michael received the call to tell them otherwise.

Catherine's return to an empty house after delivering Keira to the station left her low and dispirited. Her reflex was to pull out Rachel's cell phone to reread her texts, as had become a habit. But this time she paused, holding the phone in her upturned palm, as if it were a talisman to bring her luck for her next move. She was lightheaded, perhaps because she was hungry. She had skipped breakfast and only had coffee because Keira had already eaten by the time she came down; the remnants of her toast with its horseshoe bites sat on a plate in front of her. It occurred to her that she should make herself an omelet. Thanks to Judith, who kept Bantams, she had a supply of eggs, and she also had rosemary, which her neighbor left hanging in posies outside the French doors. She was reaching up to unhook a pan from a hanging rack of utensils with her left hand when she jogged Rachel's phone from her right. The phone hit the counter and bounced onto the limestone floor, where it smashed.

Within a matter of weeks Rowan was into the rhythm of the term. There were late nights having random conversations with Chloe in her room, listening to Radiohead and Bowie, joined by Dido and Hannah, who twisted up their hair into haystacks using claw clips, while eating lemon-cream wafers, which were sort of disgusting and sort of delicious. Sometimes he felt like their pet whippet: greeted by cries of affection when he entered, forgotten by the time he had taken his place at the foot of the bed. This was fine, as he'd go into his own zone and as soon as the subject landed on the fuck factor of his peers he'd tune out anyway; he liked their openness as a change from the girls he knew in London who were so arch and self-conscious they were psycho parodies of themselves. There was the morning race for breakfast before the surly ladies who ruled the dining hall snatched the Frosties away—he never got enough sleep to hear his alarm. Then there were the sessions with Ms. Lakme, whose probing questions were starting to be obnoxious. He blanked her when she started asking about "sexual relations." Even if he had no interest and no action, it was none of her business and he was going to make sure that it stayed that way. He quickly sussed out his teachers; who was checked in and who had checked out. Soon he had a sense of what was expected—not an awful lot compared to the pressures of his last school. There was one teacher, Mr. Douglas Stewart, who made an impression. He was there at the beginning of term and disappeared for another several weeks. Rowan was about to drop his class because the sub was truly *sub*, but fortunately Douglas Stewart returned just in time.

Douggie Stewart was known by the students for his informal style. He was tall with stooped shoulders and stalked around campus, hands plunged deep into the pockets of a wide-shouldered suede jacket. In class he was known for his dramatic delivery and wooden posture. During a lecture he would lean forward, folding and unfolding his torso like a marionette—the kids liked to imitate him and exaggerated his chopping hands for comic effect. If he wasn't ex–rock and roll, he was definitely ex-something. With hollow cheeks, lines scored vertically as if they had been put there by a razor blade, he gave the impression of having lived a lot. He was low key until he became animated, and then he would unleash with the zeal and passion of a reformer.

"There was a time when this class could have been about the land. We could have talked about topography, geology. I might have done a little unit on navigation or crop rotation, which, believe it or not, is what we did back in the day.

"As we confront a global catastrophe, there's only one conversation to be had: it's about climate change, and we'll use that as a jumping-off point to talk about land use and conservation of the Earth's finite resources. We will look at the science behind global warming. What is climate? How do our ecological systems work? How are they changing? For your first assignment, I will ask you to do something unusual, I will ask you to use your laptops"—he unfolded to full height, as if he was about to say something amazing—"for research. Yeah, I know, that's radical."

He seemed gratified when one of the girls giggled.

Rowan didn't laugh. He was rapt.

"I want you to look at the causes of climate change. I will ask you to come up with a list of preventative measures on a domestic scale—home or school if you want—anything we can do to reduce our carbon impact. Also, I want you to start thinking on a national scale. Most importantly—and here's the rub—I want you to consider why it's taking us so long to cop to the potentially catastrophic effects of warming: acidification of the oceans, rising sea levels, loss of coastal habitats, biblical weather, destruction of the polar icecap, to name a few. I want you to ask yourself why, in the face of ruin, human beings are incapable of adapting their behavior. What is the nature of this colossal denial? Are there Darwinian principles at play? Are our brains too small to make the connection between our actions and what's happening to the planet, and so we must perish because we are unfit custodians? Is there another mind-set conditioning the continuation of foolish choices—our unredeeming selfishness? To most of you this incremental rise in tempera-ture doesn't sound dramatic—what's a couple of degrees here and there? But these temperatures have been averaged, and we haven't taken into account a cycle of acceleration. Think about it. When you lose huge expanses of ice, you lose the ability to reflect heat. In your research, you will read about the *tipping point*, the moment at which the trajectory towards warming becomes irreversible. You'll hear different numbers floating about: this will happen in three years—you'll be lucky if you hear five, but every year we learn that the situation is worse than we thought. For the purposes of this class, and for your future as conscious beings, I wouldn't be scaremongering to suggest to you that the tipping point is now."

Someone dropped a book dramatically. Someone groaned, *Today? Bummer.* The seriousness of the situation filled Rowan's head, seeming to displace the oxygen along with it. He was stifled with panic and longed for air. He would have left the room because he was suffocating, but he stayed to listen to the discussion instead; he didn't want to give the wrong impression by bolting out. Someone asked, "If we misjudged everything now, what makes you think we can make anything right in the future?" This provoked an argument between the scientists and the pseudo-skeptics, which Mr. Stewart mediated with a winc-ing glee. Fortunately, the bell rang soon enough and Rowan was able to follow the flow of students before realizing they were going to the cafeteria. The idea of eating at a time of crisis seemed indulgent, so he veered to the library, running across the quad, up the steps of the new building, recently renovated to resemble a Soviet bunker. Lungs bursting, he realized how unfit he'd become since dropping cross-country. He slow jogged his way to the bank of computers, and searched "acidification of the ocean" once he had sat down. He was shocked when over 2 million entries came up. He read the first few, learning that people had been talking about the destruction of the coral reefs for a while, but in the meantime, man-made CO_2 had been steadily dissolving into the ocean. While this had the effect of slowing absorption into the atmosphere, it had been to the detriment of sea life as CO_2 was forming carbonic acid, raising the pH level, and changing the ocean's chemistry, so that shellfish were struggling to do their most basic function: reproduce and grow. The idea of a dumb mussel struggling to form a shell was so mind-blowing and pathetic that Rowan knew that something had to be done. By the time the first afternoon bell had rung to call him to his art elective, metalwork, he had different priorities. He had been hammering a copper bangle and planning to enamel it in a deep blue color, maybe do a cool astral pattern as well, but he saw how frivolous that was when so many of the most naturally perfect things were being eroded by the sea that housed them. Mr. Stewart was right: the tipping point was now.

He sprinted back to the science block, to Stewart's classroom. Running was less painful once he had found his stride and remembered to breathe. His teacher was perversely technophobe and had made it known that he preferred the spoken word as his chosen method of communication—failing that, handwritten notes, but never emails because they wouldn't be read. He had a drop box for notes inside the classroom door that would be checked twice a day. Rowan intended to leave a note requesting an appointment where he could be sure to have his teacher's undivided attention. He had so many questions. There was so much more he wanted to know.

The door was wide open.

Mr. Stewart was at his desk, hunched over a plate of food, munching while reading a journal that was propped nearby on a pile of books. Rowan hovered in the doorway, eyeing the fish and mushy peas from the Friday menu, awkward at having interrupted his teacher's lunch.

He stopped chewing and looked up with a friendly *hello*. His lips parted to reveal a layer of translucent green on his front left incisor, where the shell from a mushy pea had lodged, giving him a piratical air. He seemed to know it was there, as he picked out the debris with his finger. "Do you know that within fifty years," he continued, "there won't be enough food or water to sustain human life. However, if we all converted to veganism for more efficient land use, there's hope. Needless to say, the memo hasn't reached Canterbury Downs." He jabbed at the fish with his fork. "Besides," he said, chewing, "I never met a piece of battered cod I didn't like."

"Shall I come back later?" Rowan asked. "When you're—"

"No," Stewart said, pushing away the plate. "What can I do for you? . . . It's Rowan, isn't it?"

Rowan nodded. It pleased him that Stewart knew his name. This was only the second time they had met. "You said if we ever had questions—" He broke off. He had so much respect for this man, it was making him shy.

"Last year I gave my speech about water shortages and some selfish bastard wanted to know how that might impact his holiday in the bloody Bahamas. As long as it's not that, I'm yours."

Rowan thought of Merhan's swimming pool and the memory twisted in his heart. He told himself nothing else mattered. This conversation was meant to be. He stepped forward into the room. "I want to know what to do," he said.

Then he couldn't help it: he burst into tears.

Catherine hadn't seen Aggie Mackay in a while; she guessed in about sixteen months. When they'd last met, Aggie had just won the prestigious TBA prize, a grant from the wireless telephone company, and had moved from her mother's bungalow in Portaferry to an artists' co-op in Deptford. She was still in the process of adjusting to the shock of her good fortune and the separation from an alcoholic girlfriend. Aggie loved her new situation, part of a converted fishermen's warehouse, a block away from the river. She'd always lived near water and fancied herself as "a bit of a mud-lark," a reference to her childhood combing riverbanks, picking over stones and debris that she used in her first assemblies. She said that the local market sold the *mother of all black puddings*, where she could eat for three quid as if she still lived in Northern Ireland without having to be there. She had offered to take Catherine to lunch there, but Catherine was always busy and never had made the time to go with her.

When Catherine had last visited the studio, it was little more than an empty space. In the interim, it had filled to capacity and now brimmed with projects, tools, materials, and construction paraphernalia with the *Soulmap* center stage.

Catherine walked slowly around the perimeter, a mountain range, ten by ten, and three and a half feet high. It was built from wire and papier-mâché newsprint and thickly sealed in a dark yellow lacquer. She was silent to allow Aggie to deliver a commentary in a halting Ulster burr.

"As you can see I've been experimenting with a new resin. It's thicker than what I usually work with but it has a more of a, y'know, multidimensional quality . . . It's a devil to use—almost dry before it leaves the can."

Aggie rubbed her ears. Her hands were chafed and scratched. She never used protective gloves, as she didn't like having any barrier between her skin and the materials.

"But I'm liking the way it takes. It's more dense, y'know. Deeper. And I'm quite content with the effect of the larger scale, which we'd talked about, you might ha' suggested, and the repetitions, crag upon crag . . . Thought it was a good sign cus when I was doing the construction, instead of worrying, how was I gonna make *another effing peak*, I was juiced all the while because all the time I was building I was thinking of infinity."

It was true that Catherine had suggested the larger scale. When Catherine had first seen images of Aggie's reliefs, body parts emerging from collage that bridged the gap between two-dimensional works on paper and multidimensional sculpture, she'd been so captivated that she'd taken the first available flight to Belfast City Airport, to find Aggie in a shed at the bottom of her mammy's yard, past a pig pen and an enclosure with a mangy Connemara pony. There Catherine had seen the promise of the original *Soulmap*, although she had thought the scale too small to contain all its ideas. She had encouraged Aggie to expand and develop its physical mass, discussing with her the possibility of including a larger version in a group show. She also had been taken with Aggie's *Home* series, consisting of ordinary items—a woman's shoe, bread bin, toaster, blender— all coated in her ubiquitous resin. Catherine was impressed by Aggie's ability to objectify her pieces, harnessing the properties of the mellifluous honey-lacquer, using it like amber to suspend and capture her entities in time. Catherine had bought the entire *Home* series, in the belief that post-exhibition there would be interest in this unknown artist and it would make for a good profit.

By the time Catherine completed her rotation, she had seen that the construction was lifeless and didn't work. Gone was the dynamic expression of the smaller piece. This large version had the inanimate look of a topographical model from the Museum of Natural History. Aggie's experimental resin was as hard and dark as treacle; where the surface might have heightened, or added depth, it had deadened and embalmed. Catherine realized that by asking her to focus on the natural world, she had directed her away from her urban, working-class upbringing, for which her *Home* appliances were a commentary on feminine roles, domesticity, and her mother's aspiration. She had asked her to put on hold her most potent memories, the

curdling inhibition of growing up gay and Catholic in a paro-
chially homophobic, Protestant neighborhood, and steered her
away from a personal geography and history that had given her
work its dimension and substance. She saw immediately that
this had been a mistake.

Catherine paused to consider. There was a time when she
would have said what she thought. She wouldn't have hesitated to tell Aggie Mackay to go back and reformulate the
construction without the ugly varnish. She would have had
no trouble dealing with the artist's disappointment, resent-
ment, anguish at the waste of months of effort and the torture
of being asked to destroy in order to build again. Catherine
would have insisted on the primacy of her vision, formed by
instinct, shaped by experience.

Aggie looked at Catherine expectantly. Her eyes were pinky
red and as vulnerable as an animal's to slaughter. Her rosaceous
skin could have been mixed from the same bloodshot palette,
aside from a splattering of warm brown freckles, the color of a
giraffe's pelt. Any likeness to the tall mammal ended there, as
she was stocky and short.

Aggie sensed her ambivalence. Catherine Hall always knew
what she liked, said what she thought, made people cry with her
exacting standards, and was taking way too long to respond.

Doubt crossed Aggie's face like a shadow.

"What are you thinking, Catherine? Are ye not liking it?"
she asked.

The answer was no, but Catherine didn't say so because she
was asking herself whether that mattered. Time and time again

her judgment had proven unsound. Why were her opinions about art any exception? Perhaps she just wasn't seeing it and had become a Medusa so that everything she looked at turned to stone—the obliging artist had only done what she was told. Catherine asked herself whether she had to like a work to sell it. Half her clients saw art only in the context of the C. Hall Gallery: as long as it had the imprimatur of her name, this was enough assurance that the investment was blue chip and would return. If they didn't care or understand what they were buying, why should she? Aggie Mackay had toiled to execute her vision with her beaten hands and heart; who was to say that wasn't enough? The sculpture was imposing and had impact. Catherine imagined it in the middle of a large living room, a conversation piece, with a price tag of £100,000 in her mind it was already sold. If the act of survival was a compromise, why shouldn't art be as well? There were already too many tears in the world to make more.

"On the contrary." Catherine spoke slowly, improvising her answer. "I'm loving the boldness of scale that's unafraid to announce what it is . . . that is, in itself, an important statement about identity." This was true; size, in combination with a landlocked quality, did give the *Soulmap* a melancholic dignity. "I want you to keep going with this series, make sure that you map every place you have been. Do you think that this is something that would interest you?"

Aggie gave a sly, interior smile. With her red eyes, she looked quite diabolical. "That's a lot of resin, Catherine. Do you know how old I am? I'm going to be twenty-eight soon."

Catherine laughed as if to say, *Nonsense, you are a baby.* "Lewis will be in touch to make arrangements and help get you anything else you need."

"You'll have to let me take you for lunch at the market when you're next here. We'll have that black pudding I was telling you about. You're probably thinking offal is awful, but trust me, by the time it's meltin' on your salty tongue it will have changed your world."

"Change my world? I like the way that sounds," Catherine said. "We have a deal."

He was only a second into a version of the dream. He and Rachel were camping, this time they were in a snowy wilderness. She was leaving the tent—not the luxe, glamping number of his dream before, but a basic tarp strung across a pole, open at the sides and flapping in the wind, leaving them exposed and cold. He knew that this was the last time he would see her and had so much to tell her about what had been going on since the accident, although in the parallelism of dreamtime he was keenly aware that her death hadn't happened yet. When he tried to say something, he couldn't speak. No words would come out: he was paralyzed and choking with emotion. When he was jolted awake by his mobile—his mother calling—he was glad to get up, talk, and breathe. She informed him that she was coming to school the next day to take him out to dinner. She would organize a weeknight exit pass. Could he please book a restaurant and choose somewhere nice? They could go anywhere he wanted. The interruption was also a good moment for Rowan to ditch the wet towel. After returning from the showers, he had fallen asleep—probably the first time since starting at Canterbury Downs that he'd been anywhere near his bed before midnight.

The timing of her visit wasn't great. He already had plans but didn't mention them; he wasn't likely to be given any choice in the matter. At the beginning of the weekend the students congregated in Stewart's rooms and it was good fun, a party without alcohol. Mr. Stewart provided apple juice, hummus, cheese, and crackers, paid for out of his own pocket, as it was an unofficial gathering. What made these evenings work was that anyone could come. No one was excluded and there was none of the usual hierarchical bullshit to get in the way. This made for an upbeat mix: everyone was encouraged to be vocal and almost no subjects were off-limits— culture, teachers, politics. Stewart took a backseat but kept enough control to make sure that nothing too outrageous happened that could be reported and bring him reproach. When Stewart heard Fred boasting about how many spliffs he had stockpiled for later, he motioned Fred to step outside. When they came back in, Fred was quiet, humble, as if he'd been corrected. There were some kids who didn't get what the evening was about. They came and ate from the spread and left without talking to anyone. This pissed Rowan off because their behavior was against the spirit of the evening. He was surprised that Mr. Stewart never said anything but sat in a collapsed armchair, impassively watching the juvenile prats come and go. Rowan was convinced that he was a seer, that he could look to the future and tell that what they had coming was going to be retribution enough.

Rowan chose a local pub, the Tudor Arms, for their meeting, even though Kitty warned him that the food was ratchet. This was a compromise, to walk there and get back earlier, rather than drive all the way to Canterbury in search of better cuisine. He wasn't that bothered about eating; his mother was much more likely to care. On the nights she didn't go out, she used to make complicated dinners, lost on him and Rachel, who didn't like herb-drenched sauces. But Rowan disliked waste as much as he did her cooking and always made an effort to get something down. His father was always the first to make appreciative noises—Rowan couldn't tell if he was humoring her as well. Often Rachel would refuse to eat, and there would be a tense standoff between mother and daughter, with Rachel leaving the table to graze on cereal and Catherine frustrated because she thought Rachel was being obstinately ungrateful of her efforts to put good food on the table. Rowan was with Rachel on this one. As he and Rachel would have been happier eating bread or pasta, as they did whenever possible, it seemed their mother could have saved herself a lot of effort by recognizing this simple fact.

Rowan waited by the bar, sizing up the medley of agricultural workers' tools and memorabilia on the walls, relics from a time before the invention of new industrial exploitations. There were photographs of hop pickers in Sunday best with white-smocked children; their poverty and hardships temporarily scrubbed away to create a decorative genre of quaint rural nostalgia for consumption by the new nineteenth-century urban society. These sentimentalized portraits were offset in the pub by the rank smell of yesterday's beer. When some lads swaggered in carrying pecs and biceps, seriously *built*, followed by their girlfriends in miniskirts and high heels, Rowan retreated to the dining-room alcove occupied by a silent, elderly couple to avoid their loud banter and being seen as the weedy voyeur he sort of was.

He glanced at the menu. Nothing inspiring: fish and chips, hamburger, veggie burger. He settled on the latter. He was having a go at being vegetarian, but so far finding his options limited. Ozzy had a point when he said there weren't many concessions made for vegheads. His mother wasn't going to like the menu, but then she wasn't driving several hours for the food. On the phone she'd said, *There's something I need to talk to you about*, as if she had news that could only be delivered in person.

He ordered an orange juice and speculated on what that something might be.

His first thought was that his parents were getting a divorce. That was most likely. They were polar opposites. He couldn't remember any joy or physical affection between them; that only existed in photographs taken when they were young. Even those pictures were not trustworthy documents. As his research was teaching him, photographs were framed to create impressions; often designed to obfuscate and lie.

By six thirty p.m. his mother still hadn't arrived. He texted her to find out where she was as they were meant to meet at six.

Waiting for a reply, he wondered if she had been in an

accident. She wasn't a great driver at the best of times—all jerky starts and stops, heavy on the brake pedal. He remembered being in the car with her. They were going through the village after leaving Grandpa's funky commune, and she'd almost knocked over a man on a bicycle. The cyclist had seen them coming and swerved to avoid being hit. Rowan would never forget the shock on the man's face as he registered what might have happened if it hadn't been for his sharp reflexes. After she pulled back onto the road, leaving the cyclist to curse at her, arms waving—with his helmet, bum padding, and skinny Spandexed legs, he looked like an angry beetle—she'd apologized to Rowan with a sheepish smile, *That won't ever happen again,* and he'd thought at the time, more likely it would.

He acknowledged the possibility of an accident and let it go. Without confirmation, he wasn't giving the idea any more space in his head.

His phone vibrated her reply: *Qill be there 7ish as arranged.*

What planet was she on? She was already thirty minutes late!

He didn't text back, as he wanted her to focus on the road ahead.

While sipping his drink, he concluded that divorce was the most likely scenario. That wouldn't be such a tragedy. He was sorrier for her that she had to drive all the way to tell him what he already knew.

By the time his mother strode into the pub, looking as if nothing was the matter and as though she owned the place, Rowan had been alone at the Tudor Arms for over an hour. He'd watched the pumped-up group at the bar go somewhere else for more raucous fun, his companions in the alcove *fossilize* before his eyes, and he'd endured the sympathy of the waitress, "Been stood up, have you, luv?" she'd asked after his third orange juice, second bag of crisps. All the while he'd been wondering what he'd been missing at Stewart's. They bickered about whether the rendezvous had been at six as he'd understood, or seven as she insisted; she was convinced that she was only ten minutes late because of traffic.

"Agree to disagree?" He sounded like his father. This was what he said in family squabbles. She never was going to admit that she was wrong.

"Agreed." She was equally eager to make peace. "We mustn't waste any more time arguing."

There followed a general inquisition about school, which he contrived to answer as generally as possible. He had to wait until the food was on the table before she would say what was on her mind. He'd ordered a veggie burger and she'd vaguely asked for "the same."

"I'm thinking of taking a lodger," she finally told him. "Obviously, I wouldn't make such a big decision without consulting you and finding out what you feel about this, or whether you have any concerns."

"A lodger . . . wow." Rowan was stumped. Although he hadn't been diligent about staying in touch, he'd maintained a comfortable perception that everything at home was the same as when he'd left. It was a definite adjustment to think that things were going on there without him knowing. "How will you go about finding someone?" He finally thought of something useful to say.

His mother hesitated. "I already have. A young woman. Someone in need."

Rowan paused.

Again, her answer required a mental shift. Her plan was further evolved than he would have supposed.

"*Right.*"

"She would need to have Rachel's room. I want to make sure you are completely comfortable with this."

Now he understood why she was being so awkward.

Rachel's room; that colorful emporium, mysterious repository of *stuff*: makeup, jewelry, clothes bursting out of drawers and cupboards. He couldn't imagine where it had all come from and how she'd managed to get so much of it.

It was weird to think of someone occupying her room. Yet it didn't exist anymore as he knew it, so he wasn't sure why the idea of someone lodging there was disturbing.

"Sounds like a good idea. Why should I mind?"

"I don't know . . . but I do think it's important for you two to meet before we make a decision."

Rowan balked. The idea was creepy. "I don't need to meet her."

"I wouldn't let her move in without you meeting her first," she insisted. "I would never do that to you," she added, somewhat dramatically.

He could feel her will, pressuring him to agree. He hated the way she did that. He wasn't even going to be around, yet there she was, trying to impose a virtual stranger on him. "I told you it's a great idea. I don't need to meet her. The house has way too big a carbon footprint for a family of two. Why not make it three?"

His mother's face crumpled and she suddenly looked as if she were a hundred years old. He had wanted to rebuff her but not that much.

"Look, if it makes you feel better I'll meet her."

Her expression lifted. "Thank you," she said with emotion. She was pathetically grateful. "You have always been such a brilliant, sensitive boy. I knew you'd understand."

Now that conversation was out of the way, she was more cheerful.

She noticed the food in front of her. She pulled up the bun and looked at the patty curiously. Rowan thought it looked synthetic and greasy and he wished he wasn't craving a cow burger. She squirted a thick layer of mustard all over the patty and began to eat with gusto. He was surprised that she could tolerate so much spicy food.

"I'll bring her to see you or you can come down to London," she said, chewing. Her eyes were watering. Real tears or mustard ones? "I think you're going to like her."

Don't think so, Rowan doubted, but kept his thoughts to himself.

The task of searching through piles of unsolicited photographs and transparencies that arrived at the gallery every week was unrewarding more often than not. Sifting through layers of derivative nonsense, reams of crudely executed crap, was something Catherine viewed with a degree of impetus and excitement but mostly duty and obligation—it wasn't every day that she discovered a gem like Aggie. In spite of disappointments in Deptford, Catherine's belief in the artist remained intact, especially as a call from a collector had confirmed her faith that *Home* would deliver many times over. During the period of her longest absence Lewis had asked to take over the "hopeful file," as he sometimes called it, but Catherine refused to delegate, trusting only her own eyes to spot diamonds in the rough. Earlier she had looked at a pair of free standing screens, micro-mosaics of colored glass, cascading geometric shapes, gradations of yellow to red, submitted by a third-year student at St. Martin's. The stained glass had a hypnotic quality that both compelled her and repelled. She had been sufficiently conflicted to reconsider her response, asking herself whether she could disentangle aesthetics from association, whether it was the churchy stained glass that was turning her off. To be diligent she put the image aside for further consideration, placing it on top of the file marked "Hold."

When Catherine started the gallery, taking out a forty-year lease on a former furniture store in South Kensington, she had divided the area into two. In the first part, she constructed the main exhibition space, with a steel-and-glass table and white leather chairs for Catherine or an employee to maintain a presence up front, subdividing the remaining space for everything else that she didn't want seen—office, storage racks, kitchenette and bathroom—into four smaller rooms in the rear. Three times a week Elsa, her accountant, came to do bookkeeping and secretarial work.

Lewis sidled through the sliding doors with a letter for signing, outstaying his welcome by noticing the mosaics, making a discerning *mmm* sound while saying something about *post-HIV rose windows*. Whilst she'd made the same connection herself, she wasn't in the mood to hand out Brownie points, and gave him a look to see him off. She was already out of sorts with him, as his lunch breaks had become ridiculously long, and peaked recently at an epic three hours. When she'd asked him to make sure he was back on time, he'd made an excuse about finessing a private collector, claiming that he'd been drumming up business for the gallery, but without any concrete result.

He walked away with his head in the paperwork, taking

small steps like a Geisha. For no good reason this annoyed her. She told herself to get a grip and stop being menopausal.

She sat there awhile, waiting for the telephone to ring.

She answered some general enquiries.

Annoyingly, some personal calls for Lewis.

She allowed her attention to wander outside. Through the wide picture window there was a view of the street. Spring had come late that year, released from the icy grip of a Siberian winter. The cherry tree had celebrated liberation with festoons of decadent blossoms and was already dropping them to make a drowsy pink bed of petals on the pavement outside. A young couple sauntered by, treading lightly without the burden of heavy clothes. They were careless. Carefree. She wondered how long it would be before they became careworn. Was anyone exempt from this progressive condition? She was surprised to see Michael walk briskly past and turn into the gallery. In profile, the features that he shared with their son were more telling: same willing jaw, playful retroussé nose, and high forehead—his becoming more so with the recession of his hairline. His unannounced arrival reminded her of when they first met. He would trot into the auction house, ostensibly a casual visitor with an interest in art, transparently a man with a crush. Amongst her younger colleagues, he was known as *gentleman stalker*. "Gentleman stalker in the house," they would stage mutter as soon as he entered the building. At first she was obliged to talk to him. It was her job to liaise with visitors and answer queries—plus there was no way of distinguishing between a casual cruiser and a serious collector. She didn't mind his inquisitions. He asked good questions and there was always a humorous undertow beneath each one. It wasn't long before she began to think about him during the intervals between his visits; soon, she realized that she was looking forward to seeing him and was waiting for his return. With his enthusiasms and incorrigibly good spirits, she liked being around him. She liked the way he made her feel.

He entered the gallery with a smile, holding up a bag with lunch from her favorite local restaurant. He'd been in the area showing a commercial space and had called ahead to find out that she was there—although that was hardly necessary. Unlike Lewis, she wasn't in the swing of doing lunches every day. From her husband's buoyant mood, she assumed the viewing must have gone well and that he had positive news to share. Only after she'd polished off with unusual appetite a Caprese with focaccia and an even more delicious insalata tonnato did she discover the true nature of his appearance. Moving the cardboard containers aside, Michael opened his briefcase and produced a photograph of his own, which he lay down before her on the table. It was one of Hamdean that he'd downloaded from the Internet, having searched thousands of sites to find.

"I knew it," he said, pointing in triumph to the center of the photograph. "There was a structure. See!"

Catherine regarded the image.

It was taken at twilight or "magic hour," as the cinematographers liked to call the diffuse, flattering light. A man stood between two beautiful women; the females draped on each arm either side. As Michael was so pleased to discover, the louche group was arranged under the canopy of a raised open-sided gazebo.

Michael tapped the man. "That's Clive, the director."

The fellow was bland and balding. He was holding a Champagne glass up and forward not so much in a toast but as if he wanted it to be seen. His self-satisfied grin told Catherine that he was gratified by the presence of two attractive women, and was something of a braggart.

Michael's finger moved to the right, to a woman in a plunge maxi-dress.

"Here's your ballerina, Marine Deveaux."

Marine Deveaux was lovely. She had graceful shoulders and a long, swanny neck. She was unhealthily skinny, though. The lines of her ribs curved across her décolleté.

His finger slid left, to Clive's other side. "Stunning mystery woman," he continued. "Don't know who she is, but it looks as though she must have been a model."

That sounded about right. Whereas the dancer had a knowing beauty, gazing down her nose, face three-quarters, chin just-so, the woman on the left was less studied, with rambling corn hair and the pretty innocence of an angel.

"And here"—Michael pointed to the bottom of the photograph—"is your friend."

In the foreground, on the edge of the platform and apart from the others, a young girl sat crossed-legged in shorts and a halter top. She was staring directly into the camera as if she were the only one who was honest enough to admit it was there.

"It's her," she whispered, seeing Keira with the years stripped away.

"Look at the topiary," Michael said, pointing at the bottom

right corner. Peeping out was a low box hedge, shaped into a square.

Good for finding robins' nests.

"Much prefer it now without," he continued.

Catherine wasn't listening. She was absorbed by the image and staring at the photograph transfixed.

Naturally, the girl's features were smaller, less pronounced than those of the young woman she'd met—her cheeks and nose had become more defined since, but her defiant eyes were unmistakably the same.

"Funny she didn't remember the summerhouse," he added casually. "It wasn't that long ago."

"Not especially," she clipped. "Look how young she is—a mere child."

"At her age I could remember most of Keats and half of Wordsworth." He shrugged apologetically for being a know-it-all.

Catherine was exasperated at his lack of imagination. "You memorized *Beowulf* to impress your father. Children don't care about property lines and posterity. Only adults care about these things."

"You may have a point," Michael said, rising from the table. He cleared away the empty containers, tipping them into the carrier bag. "Memory is suspect," he continued, "that is, all except my own." He scrunched the foil wrapping, kneading it with both hands into a ball. He took aim at the bin six feet away. "Did I tell you?" he added. "I sold a garage today."

"Sorry?" Catherine was looking at the photograph again.

"Buyer wants to knock it down to build a 'lifestyle restaurant.' That's a gym and an organic cafe, the latest in yuppie gratification, where you can eat yourself silly and then go and work out. Or is it the other way around?"

"So much for your flawless memory."

"Ah, yes . . ."

When Michael didn't move, she sensed that he was waiting for something: approbation, she assumed, as she hadn't been listening. "Good for you, on the sale."

"I suppose it is." Michael took his shot. "It's better than a kick in the teeth." He seemed cheered that his foil ball didn't miss: it went straight into the bin.

f Catherine was offhand with Michael when he visited the gallery and impatient about his investigations of the summer-house, it was because she had more serious concerns: Keira had disappeared. She was far more worried about her safety and whereabouts than the location of an ex-gazebo from the past.

Since Keira had left Hamdean, she had rarely been far from Catherine's mind. The more she thought about her situation, the more she saw how precarious it was. With no vocational training, nor a plan of any substance, she could see that Keira was in danger of drifting, coasting without landing. This could only go on for so long before she became discouraged and depressed. Then, who knew what would happen when she was vulnerable? All this could change, subject to the meeting with Paige Wells. It was possible that with their confluent interests Keira and Paige might click. If Keira was lucky, she might find her way to an entry-level job at the magazine. On the day of the interview she had itched to call Keira to find out how it had gone, but had restrained herself knowing how the young hated being crowded. She'd wanted to give her the space to respond in her own time.

She waited another twenty-four hours before calling Paige. She was aware that she was probably in the middle of a conference with Miuccia Prada, but what the heck, friendship was important too.

Paige answered on the first ring and said in a low voice: "She didn't show."

"You are joking." Catherine was shocked. When imagining different scenarios, she had not conceived this.

"Unfortunately not. She didn't even call to cancel."

That Keira wouldn't turn up to a meeting that had been set up exclusively for her benefit didn't make any sense. "Are you certain? Could there have been a mistake?"

"Not on my end. The arrangements were clear. Frankly, I was surprised since she was coming from you. Remind me who this person is?"

"Keira Martin."

"Yes, you told me her name, but I meant, who is she? How do you know her?"

"She's the child of someone who used to live here."

There was a silence while Paige waited for her to provide details of a relationship or pedigree to offset such rank behavior. When Catherine wasn't forthcoming, she unleashed: "Honestly, I am fed up with these flaky girls who think fashion is a soft option and come in here to bide their time. Don't they know how hard it is to make art out of commerce? How many years we have slogged to get to do what we do? I had Stig's daughter come to see me the other day. You remember Stig? You had dinner with him at my house. Number two and a half on all the magazines?"

Catherine had a vague recollection of a man with spiked hair talking about Fitbit and mobile sites. "I don't remember."

"Like your friend, his daughter also happens to be interested in editorial—he asked if she could come in to talk to me. Do you know that she had the nerve to lecture me about recycling trends in fashion? As if that's a novel thought, of course we are all paying our debts. She behaved as if I was an elderly relative being visited on sufferance—all this coming from a dimwit in a blouse that showed her boobs and a skirt that showed her crack. I wanted to tell her that if she thought her outfit was cutting edge she should consider a career in latex design for Slutty Apparel."

"Why didn't you?" Catherine was dry.

"Come on, Stig's daughter? You have to understand that I have people in and out of my office all day with agendas— nothing wrong with that, but these time wasters really get on my tits when there are talented and educated women out there who have passion and commitment. They may not know some-body who knows the editor, but they are much more deserving."

"I'm sure all she wanted was a chance."

"Look, I'm sorry to rant. I know you were trying to help. And I think it's good, really great that you were, but I wouldn't waste your time. She's slippery, this one. I'm sorry if that's not what you want to hear."

"Thanks for trying. I appreciate your consideration." Catherine was stiff. She didn't care if she registered disapproval.

"Anytime." Paige was matter-of-fact. "But how are you, my darling? You are elusive. When I call the number in London I get Michael, who refers me to your mobile or the number in the country. Both those mailboxes are always full."

"I should do something about that."

"And, Rowan—how is he?"

"I expect, as you might expect."

"It's going to take time."

Catherine was silent. Implicit in Paige's remark was that there was a time frame for recovery. *Does one ever recover?* In her mind recovering was synonymous with forgetting. She wasn't sure that she wanted to forget. When she had broken Rachel's phone, it had been devastating to lose a line to her daughter, a reminder of whom they both were when she had not been looking.

"Are you angry with me, Catherine? I'm getting that vibe."

"I can't talk now . . . sorry."

"I hope you're not fobbing me off? Haven't we known each other too long to—"

"We can speak later."

"Of course—but make sure next time you take my call."

When Catherine put down the receiver, her hands were shaking. Everything about the conversation had upset her: Paige's accounting of the apparent mix-up with the meeting; her tone, which had been dismissive and patronizing. It wasn't only her unflattering opinion of the young women that offended her, but what it had revealed about Paige herself—namely her monumental ego and jealousy. She didn't believe for a second that Keira hadn't turned up. It was much more likely that Paige hadn't put the meeting in her diary and the girl had been turned away from the building without an appointment. If it had been anyone else, forgetting would have been an innocent mistake, but knowing Paige it was a passive-aggressive act, stemming from an ancient rivalry that was suddenly rearing its ugly head. If she hadn't been so damming, it might have been nostalgic to see the face of competition after so many years. *Get on my tits? Showed her crack?* If anything, Paige was the vulgar one for using demeaning and hypersexualized language. If she was going to preach she needed to find a new vocabulary, especially as she was the one whose job it was to create a climate of envy for cosmetics and designer clothes, a bondage that made women more stupid for wanting them. Art out of commerce? *Give me a fucking break!* When she thought about it, she'd never liked her. When they'd first met they were both alpha females, English majors, with an interest in art. Finding themselves with the same enthusiasms in the same circles, they had allied together as a way of neutralizing their natural opposition to each other. Then Catherine switched to art history: Paige did too. When Catherine did her PhD, Paige headed straight to work for a soon-to-be-defunct art quarterly, before segueing into fashion. Looking back at the pivotal moments that a good friend might have celebrated: marriage, birth of a child, a successful show, a positive review, Paige's reaction had always been tepid. She hadn't wanted to see it before, but Paige was a draining naysayer, the kind of person who sucked the energy from the room but was incapable of giving anything back. What was most unforgivable was the way she'd used a young person as a pawn in a game of one-upmanship. Instead of admitting her own error, she had chosen to take a negative position against her. It must have been humiliating for Keira, who wouldn't have been able to go near the building without authorization. She hoped that she wasn't discouraged. She half expected the phone to ring at any moment—Keira calling to complain. She decided that she would sympathize, and then quickly move on. They would figure out a plan B—whatever that might be—she was resourceful and would think of something. When no call came, Catherine resolved to give her some time, another twenty-four hours, for the girl's dignity, before she tried telephoning. If she had been embarrassed by being turned away, it was possible she might want to put a day between a bad experience and the telling of it. Finally, she called Keira's number. A recorded message told her that the number was no longer in service. Her first thought was that she'd dialed incorrectly. After several more tries, she wondered if the girl had accidentally written the wrong number. She tried substituting the number 8 for 5, as it was only a half a pen stroke away. When that didn't produce results, Catherine began to believe the line had been disconnected because the girl hadn't been able to pay her bill. She regretted not having taken her email as well. She even considered calling Paige to check whether she had any other contact details but decided against this. As Catherine was Keira's referee, it would seem odd that she didn't have her number and would reflect badly on them both, possibly compound the negative impression that Paige already had. And so she waited, hoping the girl would make contact with her again.

Then Michael had appeared at the gallery with his bloody photograph. She couldn't be too annoyed with him. He didn't fully understand why Keira had become a sensitive subject with her—she hadn't kept him up to date with all her dealings. Even so, his pedantic quibbles were unhelpful and she didn't understand what he was trying to prove. All she wanted was another chance to see Keira again, to remedy the damage she had done by advising her to see that self-centered egotist for advice about her career.

The same day the new issue of the *Great Estates Quarterly* came out, the letter also arrived. As soon as the brochure was distributed, Michael double-checked the properties he represented—a total of six in this one, eight including the two he shared. He liked to make sure all the information was correct, just in case mistakes had made their way into the document between proofs and publication—"gremlins," as he called them, or "ghosts in the machine." All was fine, everything suitably glossed and glossy. As he leafed through the pages, it never ceased to amaze him the sheer volume of historic estates that came up for sale every year—and these were only a fraction. How impermeable they must have seemed at the time, set up with care and pride, bastions of family and success, only to be sold, dismantled, and exchanged by second and third parties, with as little delicacy or emotional attachment as players in a game of Monopoly. With a shudder, he recognized that it wouldn't be long before Hamdean went through a version of these proceedings, although since being carved up into apartments it was no longer significant enough to be included in such grand company.

At eleven, he went to reception and grabbed an espresso from the nifty pod contraption, plus two biscuits to get himself through until lunch. When he returned to his desk, he saw that Karen had delivered the morning's post. On top of his inbox there was an envelope addressed in his son's looping hand.

He speculated on its contents, guessing that it was an official form, a permission slip for signing, otherwise Rowan would have texted. He acknowledged that it was a sorry state of affairs that a mundane communication from his elusive son could evince so much excitement and be the highlight of his day.

When he sliced open the envelope, he was surprised to see that there was a letter inside—a long one at that. The sight of so many words was emotive and caught him unawares. He wasn't sure whether this was because he was witnessing the miracle of a child's consciousness, or whether it was his amazement that Rowan could read and write in an illiterate, techno age, or whether it was because the last time he received a handwritten note from him had been on Father's Day, ten years before.

After reading the letter, he was emotional in a different way.

Dear Dad,

I hope all is well with you and that everything is fine. I am writing to your office because I don't want Mum to get hold of this first and I suspect you might want a chance to prep her on what I'm about to say.

I have decided to leave school at the end of term. I have found something so much more meaningful to do with my life than smoking dope, doing A-levels, and sleepwalking through the rest of my education. I don't want to waste any more time and money when there are so many more important things to be done in the world. We are at a tipping point now with global warming and I need to do something to stop the destruction of our planet before it's too late. I can hear you groaning and urging me to stay on at school and suggesting a BA in environmental studies or emerging energies, political science or a law degree, but, trust me, I've given this a lot of thought and have gone through all my options and come to the conclusion that only urgent action will suffice. We are beyond talk. Any hope of change will be blocked by the massive corporations that run our country and have us in a toxic stranglehold, controlling the economy, the press, and government—policy is being dictated by a self-interested elite. To save the planet we must find alternatives to unjust systems in selfless community and confront those who are invested in keeping us in a cycle of pollution and greed. To do that we need people on the front line. I'm not alone. There's a group of us and we are growing. Before you freak out, ask yourself what have you taught me other than to work hard, be polite and respectful. I ask that you respect me now by taking me at my word. Please don't try to persuade me against any of this. If you do you will make it impossible for me to stay in contact and I would like to be able to talk to you and Mum from time to time.

I plan to be in touch with the lawyer who handled Grandpa's trust so I can access the money he left me so I can use the money to live on. Please don't try to stop me—not that there's much that you can do. There was a reason that Grandpa wanted me to have this money when I turned 16 and you should respect his wishes too.

I know that at first this will be hard for you to understand and I'm sorry if my decision causes you and Mum any more stress. I hope that in time you will come to see that what I am doing is for the best. Things are different than when you were born, which is why I need to do something now.

Love,

Rowan

Michael experienced Rowan's letter as an assault. Reading it was the psychic equivalent of being punched by a stranger in the solar plexus, while learning of his child's abduction by the same. In a short period of time Rowan had become remote, but there was no end to the dismay of discovering how far he had actually gone. He could have broken down and cried but office decorum at Great Estates told him that it was best to reserve that option for later.

He reread the letter. It was worse than he'd thought on first sight.

The unfamiliar language was striking. Rowan's proposed abandonment of his education to an environmental fringe was beyond the pale. This letter did not read like the gentle and tolerant boy he knew but the voice of a chippy, left-wing militant. Rowan never used words or phrases such as "tipping point," "suffice," or "come to the conclusion," and he questioned whether Rowan had written it at all or been put up to it by one of his friends or another subversive type. He wondered whether his therapist at school had been responsible for radicalizing him. He hadn't liked the last one in London who looked like Charles

Manson and hadn't even had the good manners to wear socks to the meeting. He wished that he had listened to Catherine's warnings and had stopped Rowan from going away.

The money that Rowan referenced in the letter had been controversial from the start.

Catherine heard about the money from her father when both children were still in nappies and Rachel just crawling. They had driven down to see Frank for lunch in Sussex. After noticing how old and doddery Frank was looking, Michael waited for them all to finish their ham and cheese sandwiches (the extent of Frank's culinary expertise) before leaving father and daughter inside the cottage to have time together, alone. According to Catherine, Frank had told his daughter that he was going to settle £25,000 on each of his grandchildren to have at the age of sixteen, to which Catherine had replied that was very kind but wasn't eighteen, or even twenty-one, a more appropriate age, when they would be more likely to do something worthwhile with the money? Frank had told her that she was missing the point: the money was for them to pursue a passion, give them the freedom to travel, take a trip they might otherwise not take. He knew how important this could be. After leaving art college, he'd spent two years traveling in Mexico, South America, and Japan, having scraped enough cash by sketching tourists outside Hyde Park. This period had proven the most formative of his life. When she'd tried to argue her point, he'd cut her short: "Catherine, I've seen you make choices, and they haven't always made you happy," which she'd taken about as well as a slap in the face. She'd backed off completely and made a hasty exit,

Rachel on her hip, Rowan swinging in a bassinet in her hand. She'd found Michael in the field, chatting to some ramblers he'd met on the footpath. Seeing her expression, a compelling eye-roll and glare denoting that a quick exit was necessary, they went inside, bid hasty goodbyes, and left. In the privacy of the car, Catherine shared with Michael some details of her conversation. Although she'd never asked her father to qualify what he meant by unhappy-making choices, she had taken this personally, as a deep criticism of her. She believed that because she hadn't become an artist like him and had muddied her hands in the dirty world of commerce, he looked down on her and disdained her existence. Michael disagreed. He thought if anything Frank was referring to their marriage, because Frank Hall thought he was boring—it was obvious that he did. He'd seen how his father-in-law's eyes became glazed whenever Michael tried to engage him in conversation. Frank clearly thought that Catherine could have had a more interesting life if she'd married someone else. Michael reckoned he was probably right, but also thought that it would have been hard for her to find someone more devoted. He agreed with his wife that sixteen was too young to be trusted with such a large sum of money, but he never would have had the temerity to say this to Frank. He also understood why Catherine's reaction might have seemed ungrateful to her father and he said as much to his wife.

Catherine called the lawyer who handled her father's settlement, a Mr. Durlacher, who was part of a large firm that handled family estates. Mr. Durlacher listened with a polite but professional manner, making it clear that, as she wasn't his client, he wasn't able to discuss the matter, but he did let it be known that as the children were minors there was nothing that required him to notify the child, only the parents, which was a tacit agreement that there was no need for the adults to advertise the money until the children were older. However, Rachel, being the beady one in the family, somehow found out about the legacy, presumably by rooting about in their papers. A year before she died she'd asked Michael, "What's this about Grandpa's money?" Michael had told her that it wasn't enough to make her an heiress, so she should quickly forget about it and put the idea directly out of her head. As the subject of Frank's wishes had been such a sensitive issue with Catherine, he also told Rachel that he wouldn't mention their conversation to her mother, as she would be disappointed to hear that her daughter was a snoop. Rachel had laughed and agreed. It never occurred to him to put an embargo on her sharing this information with her brother; he assumed that this was how Rowan had learned about the bequest. The deed was structured in such a way that in the event that one sibling didn't reach the age of sixteen, that child's portion would revert to the other. At the time of drafting, the paragraph outlining the worst-case scenario might have read as lawyer-speak or legalese to a layperson, but it proved prophetic and came to bear on Rachel's death, two weeks before her sixteenth birthday, when Rowan's inheritance from his grandfather doubled.

Michael decided to write to Rowan and give his son the respect that he desired. He would tell him that he would go see him on the weekend and they would sit down together, have an

adult discussion about how Rowan might realize his goals—
within the parameters of upper school. He would urge, cajole,
use every trick in the bloody book to insist that he stay where
he was and go on to university.

He was particularly troubled by the suggestion that Rowan
would sever ties if he or Catherine tried reasoning with him.
The idea that he was capable of ruthlessly cutting them off was
so painful that he wondered whether Rowan was being dramatic in order to scare him. However, the more realistic part of
him knew that his son wasn't bluffing; he had already gone and
he wasn't coming back.

He had to think how he would broach the subject with
Catherine. She was low because after a brief flurry of friendship
the girl seemed to have dropped her. She held Paige responsible
for alienating Keira, having gratuitously set her up for rejection.
The bossy editor was now completely persona non grata.

When Michael tried to analyze why he felt so bereft after
receiving the letter, he realized that he wasn't grieving for the
loss of his son—clearly Rowan was alive and would continue
to exist in the world—but for the loss of all his hopes for him,
dashed on a piece of ruled A4 paper.

The weekend at Hamdean had been too quiet and the silence was beginning to weigh on Catherine. As much as she tried to keep herself occupied with revisions and edits on the catalogue for the new show, there were still too many minutes in the day that she couldn't fill productively. Her old routine of having hours to herself for working, walking, and introspection was no longer desirable or even tenable. Michael had been coming to the house less frequently. Since he had started showing properties on weekends, he would drive to Hamdean late on Saturday night and leave again the next morning. The weekend before he had stayed in London.

He had broached the subject of selling Hamdean over breakfast on Sunday. "Can you imagine wanting to stay here long-term?"

"I don't know. I can hardly think one day forward."

"I could see us finding somewhere else—a cottage in Rye or St. Leonards. Could be a project for us, and investment."

The prospect of leaving was welcome and terrible to Catherine.

"Fewer bedrooms," she'd said flatly, but the statement was pointed. She watched his face fall, and she hated herself for making him feel that way, although part of her still thought that he deserved it, for being fickle in wanting to be rid of the home they had tried to make together.

"Yes . . . maybe thirteen months is a day too soon to make any decisions, I understand. I'm just wondering whether it's something we should consider in the near future."

Catherine didn't disagree.

Strictly speaking, she was never totally alone, as Judith was always near, with her potions, gifts, and notes. But Catherine was in no mood for friendship and scurried in and out of the house, aware that she had become a parody of herself, a character in a farce, ducking and weaving to avoid being seen. She was glad when Sunday was over, knowing that it was only a matter of time before she would be able to busy herself at the gallery and the week would start again.

On Monday, she announced to Lewis that they would finally get to grips with the press packets for the group show. Although Lewis seemed to have his own agenda that day, she'd asked him to print out mailers of all the artists' bios and reviews for the exhibition.

Lewis was a creature of habit. If he wasn't always punctual about returning on time, he was always prompt about leaving for lunch. Usually at 12:50 p.m. he would ready himself for a 12:55 departure, but her request had made him late. At 1:30

p.m. he finished the task and wound a tribal scarf around his neck (he was stylish—she had to hand him that). He transferred his wallet from his cardigan to his waistcoat while making a telephone call on his mobile. As the common area by the computers was small, it was impossible for Catherine not to overhear.

"Sorry, I got stuck here," he said, voice low with conspiracy. "Will be there in ten. Looking forward to hearing stories about roomie from hell. Don't worry, we'll have a bitch-fest and you can get it all out," he said, shutting his flip phone with a snap.

He startled when he turned and saw Catherine standing behind him.

"Excuse my French," he said, embarrassed.

"I couldn't help overhearing your conversation. May I ask, whom were you talking about?"

He hesitated, trying to gauge the nature of her request. "Oh, I was just gobbing with Melissa Goddard. You may know her dad, Bruce Goddard, who sells horses? She let a friend of a friend stay with her at her flat, God bless her soul. She was nice enough to give her a job in her boutique and the ingrate stole money and stunk up all the clothes by wearing them at night. Lissy only discovered when a customer complained."

Catherine's heart pounded. "Repeat the part about the clothes."

"She borrowed inventory from the shop. Wore the clothes. Soiled them."

"Tell me her name again."

Lewis was blank. "She didn't say."

"I need you to find out her name. Would you do that for me? It's important."

"Yes, for sure." He seemed alarmed at the urgency of her request. "I'm going to hear all the details right now." He took this as a cue to hurry away.

Catherine didn't need any further confirmation from Lewis. She was already convinced that the person he had been describing was Keira. During Keira's last visit to the house, she remembered seeing something poking out of her collar and having an urge to tuck it in, but the instinct had been almost subliminal, a detail that she had absorbed without realizing its significance. She also recalled seeing tags on the inside lapel of Keira's jacket when it was lying on the guest room chair. Hearing that someone in Lewis's extended friend group was walking around in borrowed clothes—as she visualized, price labels still on—was enough to make her connect the two women and believe that Keira and Lissy's former flatmate were one and the same.

It had to be her.

The thought that Keira was a shallow opportunist made her nauseous.

The one hundred minutes that it took Lewis to come back from lunch seemed like one thousand. Catherine sat at his desk, dialing and re-dialing variations on the number she had been given by the girl. She searched more images of Keira's family on the computer. All that came up were some images of Keira's father on film sets, peering into viewfinders and monitors, the group photograph that Michael had already found, plus some leggy glamour shots of Keira's mother, Marine Deveaux. She could only find one mention of Marine's participation in a cabaret in Nimes, making her wonder what kind of dancer Ms. Deveaux had actually been.

While she was waiting, she opened the recent documents on Lewis's computer. She didn't mistrust Lewis exactly. If he hadn't innocently flagged the situation with Keira by discussing her within earshot on the phone, she might have thought it questionable that he knew two of the girl's targets, Lissy and herself. She was just biding her time, checking to see what he had been up to that morning. Second in the files, after the gallery's press release, was his résumé, listing his education and employment history to the present day. Evidently, Lewis was planning to leave the gallery and was interviewing elsewhere. Coming on the heels of the discovery that Keira was likely a liar and thief, this was another unwelcome piece of news. With the new show in the works, Catherine relied on Lewis and depended on him for help. Given the training and responsibility she had given him over the course of two years, she would have expected him to give notice if he was intending to leave.

She was still processing the nature of Lewis's disloyalty when he returned from lunch. He seemed surprised to find her sitting in his chair and stared at her as if she were an interloper with no right to be there. Catherine registered his expression with annoyance. It was her bloody chair. She didn't pay him to job search during office hours or give her attitude.

"Did you get her name?" she asked without getting up.

"Christine," Lewis replied, still eyeing his chair.

"Christine?" Catherine queried. "Are you sure?"

"I'm giving you the information exactly as it was given me."
He was peevish now, offended at being second-guessed.

Catherine stood, allowing him to reclaim his chair. He
sidled into his seat and turned to face his computer. He made a
show of checking emails.

The fact that she was calling herself Christine didn't con-
vince Catherine that she wasn't Keira. If Keira was a user, or
worse, a professional scam artist, it was likely that she would be
using multiple names. She said nothing further to Lewis on the
subject. If he was leaving, she couldn't count on him anymore.
Nor did she mention that she had found his résumé: to confront
him about his intentions might force the issue and push him
to resign. She didn't want to do that until she had lined up his
replacement.

Lewis couldn't stay silent for long. He swiveled around to
face her. "When she moved out she left the taps on and blocked
the toilet with"—he grimaced—"you don't want to know. Can
you imagine that someone would repay human kindness that
way? Unbelievable!"

Michael's initial impression of Canterbury Downs had not been positive. When he had toured the school with Rowan, he couldn't help comparing it unfavorably with the perfectly good one that Rowan wanted to leave in London. With an arts-laden curriculum, he didn't think that Canterbury Downs gave sufficient weight to the core academic subjects. He wondered about the standard there and worried what impact its deficiencies and imbalances would have on his son. Having seen some grungy potheads lurking around campus, he had serious misgivings about the potential influence of the peer group. However, beggars couldn't be choosers: Rowan wanted to transfer at a time when most places wouldn't consider entry midterm in the year. They had to make a decision quickly so that Rowan would have somewhere to go. Canterbury Downs—CD as it was known by the students—seemed like a better option for him than having no school at all.

As Michael had promised by return of post, he drove up

to see Rowan at the first opportunity. He'd made an executive decision not to mention anything to Catherine, hoping that a quick intervention would render that conversation unnecessary. Fortunately, Catherine was at Hamdean and he was in London, enabling him to avoid being asked where he might be going so early on a Saturday morning.

Once he was on the motorway and copse replaced asphalt, and cows in pasture seemed to outnumber the worries projected ahead, he began to feel more optimistic about the meeting. To the triumphal chords of the *Emperor* Concerto he rehearsed the advice he was intending to pass on to his son. By time he heard the Rondo, he had reached Kent. Stimulated by the exultant rapport between piano and orchestra, he had almost convinced himself of Rowan's success and could practically visualize him in his robes, hood, and hat, receiving a first-class honors degree on graduation day.

The final approach to the school was scenic through fields of barley. He saw that the heads were curled, still green and pliant, and as springy as caterpillars on a stalk. Within a matter of months, the stems would dry a golden brown before being razed—then the area would look as though it had been stampeded by a herd of giants. In the duration between the taking of the slain husk and the new cycle of plowing and planting, there would be a hush much like the observance of the fallen, but it would be a deceptive stillness, a fallow cunning. For all human toil and machination, the earth was the true master of the harvest (here, his imagination was pagan): the regeneration of the soil would have already begun.

Soon a proscenium gate marked the end of arable land and the beginning of the playing fields. As the stark white modernist geometry of the school came into view, he was delighted to see there was a football match in progress out in front. As soccer had always been a passion, watching *Footytube* on his computer an essential part of his nightly routine, he pulled over to the side of the road and rolled down the window to watch.

A motley group of players jogged in opposing directions across the pitch. They wore no uniform to distinguish sides; Michael rightly assumed they were CD kids playing one another. The teams were equally matched. Both had aggressively agile forwards who seemed to take defeat and triumph with equal good humor, even allowing for some outbursts of colorful language. Some female students lolled on the grass nearby. When a midfielder kicked the ball wide toward the road, one of the young women jumped up to retrieve it. Seeing Michael inside his car, the young woman smiled before grabbing the ball, with a lift of her chin that made him think of Rachel, and a familiar sensation tightened in his chest.

On the way to the dorm, he passed through Main Hall. There was an exhibition of students' crafts, paintings, and metalwork displayed in glass cases. Michael stopped for a few minutes to look around. He saw some sensitive pencil drawings, graphics, and filigree bracelets that could easily have been for sale in a shop on Bond Street. One enamel cuff stood out, as it had swirling lunar patterns against a firmament of blue that reminded him of Van Gogh's *The Starry Night*. On a second look, he was amazed to see Rowan named as the maker. He had no idea that he possessed such skill, doubtless inherited from Catherine's side of the family, as it hadn't come from his.

Now that Rowan wanted to go out into the dangerous world, he realized what a safe haven this progressive, liberal-arts institution had been. He saw that the kids he'd perceived as wacky were the normal ones for doing teenagery things such as having bad clothes and hair. They were not undisciplined, merely unpretentious and comfortable in their skin. If anything, Rowan was the strange one for choosing to do something so precipitous as wanting to leave this refuge of creativity and peace.

Michael navigated a warren of passages and doorways to find Rowan in his room, a basic box with a bed and sink, but it had been hung with newspaper cuttings, photographs of oceans and trees, environmental action slogans, lists of events, statistics, and programs. He noticed that there were no personal photographs anywhere: nothing that would have indicated that Rowan was part of a family.

After an awkward embrace, he sat on Rowan's bed while his son took a seat opposite him on a chair. He didn't waste time. He launched straight into a pep talk about the importance of higher education. It wasn't a bad speech. He might have gone so far as to call it a rousing one. He explained that education wasn't just a diploma to ensure future employment and a larger salary, but an essential part of a young adult's moral and spiritual development. Higher learning wasn't just an intellectual journey but one of enlightenment, discovery, and hope.

Rowan listened with his head bowed. Michael hoped that

his posture was an indication of respect and a sign that his son was taking his words to heart. Yet, as soon as Michael had finished, Rowan looked up and asked, "If I leave school, what do you think is going to happen?" Rowan's question left Michael speechless. His immediate reaction was: *You will die at the hands of police thugs or end up living toothless and destitute under a bridge,* but unlike the lawyers who executed Rowan's grandfather's settlement, he didn't want to articulate his fears: that would have been to empower them, maybe even bring bad luck—the latter was irrational, he understood. He was taken aback because when Rowan had looked at him, there was an expression on his face that he'd never seen: a fervid combination of passion and sorrow.

Seeing his father unable to answer, Rowan continued, "Whatever you think, it will be worse if I don't go."

Now that Rowan had raised the subject, Michael could more comfortably say, "You will stay safe, won't you? I mean, it's all peaceful, isn't it?" He knew that by asking he was conceding defeat.

For a moment, Rowan looked incredulous.

"I'm not even going to answer that question," he said, ending the conversation.

Rowan checked his watch. He told his father that he was due in the library for a group project but insisted on walking him to the car. Although Michael didn't want to make him late, he didn't object, knowing his son's good-natured company would go a long way to sweeten the bitterness of having to leave.

On the way, Rowan asked about the lodger. "How's she working out?"

"Who?" Michael was confused.

"The woman."

They looked at each other, puzzled.

"Did I miss . . . ?" Michael wondered whether he was having a senior moment.

"Mum said you were taking in a lodger. 'Someone in need.' She wanted us to meet but never mentioned it again."

Michael realized that the ostensible boarder was Keira. Catherine must have thought about taking her in but never mentioned it, as the relationship was a nonstarter. But how precipitous and odd for her to talk to Rowan without consulting him first, but then nothing about Catherine surprised him anymore.

"Is Mum okay?" Rowan asked.

That he still cared about his mother made Michael hope that he and Catherine might not have lost their son entirely. "She's busy at the gallery. Back on track. Much better now." He didn't know if this was true, but he had to believe it.

When Michael reached the car, he sank into the driver's seat. It occurred to him that this was the last time that he would visit his child at school. As this reality hit him, he was overcome with wistfulness. He realized how much he was going to miss all the open days, plays, concerts, and conferences that had been the happy substance and framework for so many years. Without them, he wasn't sure whether life could ever seem so grounded or constructive. With a startle, he remembered Rowan's cuff. He'd been so preoccupied with own his agenda that he had failed to mention it. "I saw your bracelet in the exhibition. It's excellent quality. Really very well done. Perhaps, if you stayed on, this is something you could pursue?" He could hear how improbable this was and how unconvincing this must sound.

Rowan smiled indulgently as if to say, *Oh that.* He leaned down, squeezed his father's shoulder, and produced a folded piece of paper from his pocket. "You can read this later if you want." For Michael, "later" was within five minutes, parked between a fuel truck and a camper van, sitting at a petrol station a couple of miles away. He couldn't wait to see what his son had written.

> *Sixteen Years*
> *I have glinted*
> *and darted*
> *in a swollen sea*
> *through blooms of algae*
> *diverting me*
> *(Does being a bottom feeder come naturally?)*
> *But I rise*
> *in the wake of an expiring day*
> *I want to add more*
> *a better way*

Michael read the poem and was affected by his son's words. It moved him deeply that Rowan had chosen to express himself in this form; the verse traced an evolution from the embryonic piece that he had read at his sister's funeral to the personal direction he seemed to have found. With simple imagery and rhyme, he had managed to evoke the challenges of navigating a changing world. Writing in a language that Michael could understand, it was as if Rowan were trying to help him by letting him read his poem, saying, *See, Dad, it isn't that complicated. This is who I am.*

His next mission was to go to Hamdean, to relay to Catherine all that he'd seen and heard. Knowing how Rowan's plans were likely to be received by his mother, he wasn't relishing the task. For this reason, he opted to take the more circuitous route to the house via Staplehurst. He had read about a church there that carried a rare example of eleventh-century ironwork on the door. With the pressure mounting on him to deliver Rowan's news to Catherine, there had never seemed a better moment for him to stop and see.

The South Door was indeed remarkable. It was worth the detour to find something of that antiquity extant: a swirling Norse serpent in conflict with Thor, with the cross of Christianity presiding above. After marveling at the artistry, he entered the church, staring up at the simple tie-beam and kingpost roof, noting in admiration how the pillars along the aisle leaned to compensate for the staggered foundations. He lowered himself into a pew to get a vantage of the nave. Once seated, his thoughts began to settle and he became aware of how roiled and agitated he was. Being alone in this ancient place of worship steadied and calmed his senses. The act of being still quieted him, enabling him to stop looking and turn his gaze inwards.

He thought of his father, who was devout in his daily observance of a traditional Anglican faith. He had tried to foster in Michael an understanding of the sanctuary of rituals, taking him to matins once a week and to communion on Sunday. Yet, as an adult, Michael had become a more common kind of Christian who stepped into church only for baptisms, marriages, and funerals. Half in the water and half out, Michael had paddled safely in the shallows of agnosticism, keeping his options open whether to retreat back to the shore or wade in deeper. Instead of this giving him the leeway he desired, he had been left stranded on a spit of limbo; events of the last thirteen months had rendered freedom pointless. The last time he had been in church was at Rachel's funeral, where he had endured the agony of the service, from the gathering at the beginning, to the committal of her body at the end, without the comfort of belief or nonbelief.

He wondered what his father would have made of his situation with Rowan. They hadn't known each other; his father had died before the children were born. He reckoned that he and Rowan would have liked each other. They had much in common. His father had given himself to the service of his students. Rowan was kindred in his modesty and selflessness.

Michael remembered the excitement in the household when one of his father's ex-students, Dominic Sperry, had sent word to tell him he was coming to visit. This was Dominic's first time back at St. Christopher's since leaving ten years before. Michael's mother went into a flurry of tidying and polishing, unfurling lace runners like bunting. His father's contribution to the occasion was to stand by the mantelpiece, an enigmatic smile on his face, and reposition a brass carriage clock one centimeter to the left. At the age of twenty-eight Dominic already had his own TV talk show where he discussed current events and quarreled with politicians and prominent members of the arts. Yet, it wasn't Dominic's fame or success that had made Michael's father most proud but that he had *overcome difficulties*. As far as Michael could make out, most of his difficulties were parental: both had spiraled into a cycle of drug addiction and ill health. For a while it looked as though Dominic might go the same direction. Dominic would have lost his scholarship and been expelled for poor grades and cigarette smoking but for the intervention of Michael's father, who had advocated for him by guaranteeing to supervise him through his last two years of upper school. This he had done to good effect, operating a study hall in his living room, four days a week. His student graduated top of his class and went on to university. Michael's father didn't hold it against him that it had taken so long for him to return: this had not been the point of his service. He had seen need and promise and he had given his time freely.

Over tea, springy-haired Dom (as he became known) regaled the table with stories about obstreperous interviewees. A writer once punched him in the green room before passing out drunk, only to revive minutes before going on live for a riveting discourse on the subject: "Can Art Soothe the Savage Beast?" "Not in his case." Dominic grinned charmingly. "The answer was resoundingly *no!*" Far more interesting to Michael was Claire, Dom's female companion, a commissioning editor at the BBC. Claire didn't say much, but she didn't come off as passive, more that she didn't need to interpose herself into the conversation, as that hadn't been the purpose of the visit. When this elegant couple had ducked into the bungalow, he noticed how Dominic had his hand placed in the small of her back, how he looked at her while he was talking to others, which she acknowledged with a subtle curl of her lips to tell him, *Yes, I'm listening. I'll be your witness today.* After tea, Michael's mother went to the kitchen and the two men went out on the patio to laugh and reminisce, huddled over cigarettes—the only time Michael saw his father smoke. Michael was left alone with Claire at the table.

"How's school?" she asked warily.

"All right. Maths is difficult."

"Don't worry. Work hard and it all adds up in the end," she said, more reassuringly. By way of encouragement she broke a shortbread finger in half, handing one part to him and eating the other. This was pure conspiracy, as Claire had already heard his mother tell him that he had eaten his prescribed limit of three. To Michael this was as good as sex, with their lips and tongues sharing something delicious—even if it was separate halves of a sweet butter biscuit. She added simply, "Your father is a good man. He may have saved Dom's life." This was impossible to conceive: cocksure Dom being rescued by a dull old man?

When it was time for the couple to leave, Claire prodded Dom to promise that he wouldn't let so much time elapse before his next visit. (He never honored this pledge: he never returned). Michael and his parents walked Dom and Claire outside to an MG convertible. Dom swung into the driver's seat. Claire eased herself next to him. With one last farewell and a rev of the engine, Dom and Claire sped nimbly away. For weeks on end, Michael's father spoke about little other than the visit as he basked in the afterglow of Dominic's return. He chuckled approvingly while quoting the reason Dom had given for switching from English literature to PPE at university: *"I was going to read all those books in my spare time anyway."* He recounted some hilarious episode involving missing strawberries that Dominic had remembered. Michael couldn't stand to listen. He couldn't bear to see his father be so happy to be left behind when he, Michael, had wanted to go with them. Michael didn't understand why his father hadn't wanted more for himself. If he had saved Dom's life, surely he should have demanded and received more acknowledgment and thanks? Then recognition would have flowed in a continuous river of gratitude and Dom's attention would not have been allowed to divert away. When his father had waved Dom goodbye for a second and last time, Michael hadn't appreciated that his lack of expectation was humility and his acceptance was strength. These same qualities were in evidence when Michael had left home to go to university at the age of eighteen. Now that Michael was looking at having to do something similar with his own son, he wondered whether it was possible to have even a portion of his father's grace.

Over the years he had constructed an idea of himself of having achieved everything he had yearned for that day: marriage to a clever and beautiful woman, a life more interesting than his father's. Underpinning this notion was a fundamental miscalculation: a serious underestimation of the love and contentment that had been the bedrock of his parents' union, the quiet heartbeat that had motored them through most of their adult lives. He couldn't claim contentment was a defining quality of his own marriage—or likely to be one. Whatever it was and would be, it was what he had signed up for with Catherine.

Having more appreciation for his father was to understand more about the nature of faith. His father's humility had been inseparably allied to his conviction in a mysterious and divine order. Without sanctimony or self-regard, certitude had ballasted him, giving his life more heft and meaning than Michael had known. Appreciating the consistency of his father's beliefs made Michael conscious of having vacillated with his own. Even when he had most been in need, he had feared to make a choice that would put him on the wrong side of truth. He had failed to commit. This attitude struck him as cowardly. Nor was it sustainable. He needed the conviction of knowing, saying, doing. The latter was important to him. In his view, it wasn't God or priests that made churches and temples holy but the people who went to places of devotion, got down on their knees, and asked for help. Before continuing on his journey, he kneeled down and prayed for Rachel. He prayed for Rowan and Catherine, and then he asked God for wisdom and courage for himself.

He hadn't been gone from Hamdean long. It had only been a matter of weeks. He had been gone long enough to notice small deteriorations around the house: leaves and debris on the doorstep, a film of dust on the windows. Catherine had allowed the mail to accumulate again; a pile of unopened letters sat on the drum table in the hall. He was aware that his relationship to the old place was changing. Whereas before, one glance at the warm brickwork and cool lime mortar that had married in the façade for several hundred years would have uplifted and inspired him, but his fascination with history, the urge to pore over architectural details, cornices, and floorboards, had diminished and all but disappeared.

On his way inside, he leafed through the post. There was a baffling note addressed to him from Judith, asking him not to do building work after midnight, as it interfered with her circadian rhythms. As Catherine had already complained of being harassed by Judith, he supposed that Judith had finally lost her marbles and needed to take something stronger than her own herbal medicine.

Catherine had known something was up even before he'd had a chance to speak. She was standing in the kitchen wearing baggy sweatpants. Her computer lay open behind her, the screensaver dancing psychedelic swirls. "I wasn't expecting . . ." she said, not entirely welcoming, then added, "What's happened?" more urgently before he'd had the chance to reply.

He told her about Rowan's letter, his trip to Canterbury Downs, then braced himself for her reaction. Catherine alternated between astonishment and fury. She couldn't believe that he had *sneaked off* and excluded her from an important conversation. She accused him of botching the situation. If she had been there, perhaps the two of them could have made the difference? "We will never know." She would try to talk to Rowan, but since Michael had *caved in,* he had weakened her position. She blamed him for not supporting her when she'd known it was best not to let Rowan go away to school. Why had they put so much faith in people they didn't know? *The fucking shrinks.* While Michael knew that his own intentions had been honorable—Rowan had written to him directly and he had followed his lead—Michael's only motivation had been to spare Catherine more angst; but even so, he saw that going to Rowan's school alone had been a mistake. He didn't understand what had made him do it. All he could do was apologize to Catherine—and then apologize again. Once his regret had been made clear, she became calmer and less confrontational. Seeing a window for constructive dialogue, he reasoned with her in support of their son's decision. "Isn't this what his education has been about? We wanted him to learn to think for himself."

Catherine shook her head. "How can he know anything? He's sixteen."

He tried to convey how sincere and serious Rowan had been. "Being with Rowan was like being with a priest."

She was acid. "I'm sorry I haven't had the benefit of *that particular experience.*"

They tried to salvage the remainder of the evening with a semblance of normalcy. They cooked supper together: spaghetti carbonara, minus the bacon, as the fridge was empty apart from eggs that Judith had been nice enough to deliver. The mood was somber and the conversation was strained. When he asked how it had been going at the gallery, she was oblique. *Never a dull moment* was all she would say, making him think that she was withholding details as a retribution for his actions. He had no appetite for food or conflict and was the first to give up eating. While watching Catherine twirl spaghetti around on her fork— on every second rotation the pasta unraveled, she'd catch the strands and begin twirling again—he asked about Judith's note.

"I don't know what that woman is on about," she said dismissively. "I wish she would leave me alone."

It was Catherine's turn to abandon the meal. She took their plates and clattered them down in the sink.

Michael had been waiting for the right moment to show her their son's verse. As dinner was over and Catherine had returned to the table, this seemed to be as good a time as any.

As soon as she started to read Rowan's poem, she became anguished.

"Why didn't I make her come home?" She began to weep. "None of this would be happening if I had made her come home."

He understood her heartbreak. He wanted so badly to comfort her, to spare her more pain. "Darling . . . please . . . I am coming to see that what is happening is greater than any one of our actions. That she got into that car—had her life taken away—"

"Don't." She was savage. "I can't listen to any of this spiritual crap. If there's any reason she's dead, it's because of me."

"I don't think you can fairly—"

"I didn't answer her text," she snapped. "You asked her to text me, yet you have never asked me why I never replied."

In all the awfulness, it had never occurred to him to make this into an issue. He had assumed that Catherine had never received her message; that is, if Rachel had texted her at all. They had both held themselves culpable for not having made her come home, but they had never dissected the timeline of phone messages. He didn't like where the conversation was going: it was obvious, someplace dark. He tried to steer her away. "All I know is that we must be good to each other, here and now."

But she was launched on her course. "If you won't blame me, I blame you," she cried. "Why didn't you take responsibility when she asked to stay out? Why didn't you step up and be her father instead of pretending a decision about your daughter's safety was beneath your concern?"

Her words winded him. As soon as he could speak, he tried again. "We must be good to each other . . ."

"Why don't you blame me when you know she texted me that night? I opened her text—it was marked read the next day—and I didn't reply. I don't remember reading it."

He didn't know how to answer. This made no sense.

"Are you hearing me? I opened her text, but I don't remember reading it."

He couldn't stand it anymore. "I blame myself," he said loudly. From the way her eyes suddenly widened, he realized that he was shouting.

"Tell me why. Take a goddamn position."

He was yelling before he realized what he was saying. "For trusting you to make the right decision."

She let out a cry of satisfaction, but it was a wail, an animal cry, like nothing he had ever heard. He had wounded her, yet she seemed glad to have extracted an accusation.

"Are you satisfied now?" he implored. "Will you please stop?"

With a gulp, she composed herself. "You are right. You should never have trusted me."

"You know, I didn't mean . . . sometimes, you push me . . . Don't you see that it's a delusion to think that we have any control over what happens to our children? To treat them like a project with a prize for the ones with the best design? This is our hubris. All we can ever do is hope is for the best. Instead of hurting each other, we should have some humility about the limits of our capabilities, and admit that we are powerless before—"

"Please—"

"—God," he said firmly.

She stared at him as if she had been betrayed. "I do hope for the best. For all our sakes. I only want what's best for you and for Rowan. I'm sorry that I spoke so harshly to you." With that, she withdrew from the argument.

They stayed in the kitchen until it was time to go to bed. She sat there stiffly while he held her in his arms. He wanted to be close to her. He needed to be sure that they were both all right. What had passed between them had devastated them all over again. He hoped that now she had provoked him to say the worst and voiced so much guilt and rage of her own, there was a chance that finally she would be able to heal.

In the middle of the night, he woke up and he was hard. He was on his back and Catherine had already mounted him. By the time he was awake and fully conscious that he was not dreaming, he had climaxed. He felt dirty afterward, as if he had taken advantage of Catherine when she was vulnerable. Only in the morning, when he woke, uneasy in their damp bed, was he able to separate his automatic guilt from the memory of what actually had happened. He realized that during sex, which was crudely mechanical, even punishing, she had been the one taking advantage of him.

As soon as his father was on the road and safely out of sight, Rowan sprinted to the tennis court located at the end of the playing fields, where the land dropped away to meet the brim of the north woods. Stepped into a grassy slope, the area was set away from the main campus and sheltered out of sight of teachers, houseparents, and staff. Except for a small contingent that liked soccer, most of the students at Canterbury Downs were proudly unathletic. Unless stoned or tripping on acid, no self-respecting pupil would chase a ball with a racket. Rowan rightly assumed that he would have the place to himself.

He lay down along the old net line and let his legs fall wide and his arms flop from his sides. His outspread limbs made him think of Da Vinci's *Vitruvian Man*, whose iconic figure was pinned on the wall of his art classroom. This impossibly perfect man stood at the center of the universe, with all its energy and knowledge flowing through his fingertips, but he could only ever represent an ideal. The humanists had got it wrong when they put so much stock in man's capacity for reason: men and women were not rational. There was no point trying to resolve any of the world's problems without addressing this reality. In less than an hour he would be Skyping with Justice1. Justice1 had liked Rowan's theory that environmental behaviors were a primitive throwback. In a series of posts, Rowan had written that the instinct to cling to the status quo regardless of impact was a holdover from fight or flight modes, honed for over two thousand years into obnoxious habits, the breaking of which required a fundamental shift in the structures of everything. Justice1 responded to the thread, calling him *evolutionary smart.* Since then they had been messaging each other. They planned to convene at a sandwich bar in Paddington Station, although they hadn't worked out the exact details. Today he was going to meet Justice1 face-to-face via Skype—an awesome prospect. He knew nothing about Justice1 beyond a mutual commitment to activism, giving him license to imagine his new connection as alternately male and female; sometimes an interesting combo of both. There was also a chance that JI (Justice's other signature) was gender neutral or possibly a group, as JI only used the pronoun *we.* Whatever Justice1's identity, Rowan keenly anticipated the exchange. As soon as he received a message from JI, his metabolism surged and his blood pumped that little bit faster.

Rowan pushed his head and spine into the surface. The ground created a comforting resistance and the sensation of being pushed up towards the sky. A shard of gravel at the back of his skull was a useful reminder to stay present and mentally sharp. He had given his dad the impression that he had a club session, as he looked as though he needed an excuse to leave, but now he was glad to have time on his own to get his thoughts back in order before his virtual meeting.

Okay, the planet,
the planet.
Science tells:
The default geopolitical order.
It has to be radical otherwise—

His mind kept slipping. It was stupid, but his father's visit had unsettled him and he didn't know why.

Going in, he had known the conversation wasn't going to be a barrel of laughs but he had approached it as a necessity, projecting reactions based on an understanding of him as a conventionally unimaginative, forward-marching fellow. The point of writing to tell him that he was cashing in Grandpa's bequest had been to simplify the argument, make him back off and leave him to do what he would have always done whether there had been money or not. (The lawyer's letter about the legacy hadn't surprised, as he'd already overheard his parents debating it several times.) But he hadn't expected him to turn up at school looking aged and small, or to be as staunch as a backtracking snail—he had the sense that he could have squashed him with his foot if he'd wanted. His appearance was so unfamiliar that Rowan wondered whether he, Rowan, had entered a new phase of consciousness—perhaps his dad had been this way before and he'd never noticed? But as he didn't fear the physical processes that evidently stampeded at a certain stage, he didn't think this was why he was uneasy. No, the double take was how his view of his father and his mother kept shifting. Every time he looked at them they became more contradictory, fallible, and *wrong*. Now that he was making his own decisions and being separated was the new normal, Rowan couldn't understand why any of this mattered. They had always been the same: consistently inconsistent. Rachel had always said so. She had two rants: *Mum is insane* and *Dad is a muppet*. He had always thought she was being facetious, but now he wondered why he hadn't taken what she had been saying more seriously. Perhaps this was what was bothering him the most.

He had never been interested in what went on between the three of them. Rachel was manipulative and his parents willfully gullible. They had seemed well matched, so there was no need for him to take sides or to get involved. For better or worse, he had accepted this as the way they were together—at least since he had become aware enough to notice during a family trip to Rome.

His father had organized a long weekend there for half term. Always the history nerd, he had prepped them that this was to be the holiday of a lifetime. They were visiting the eternal city: if Rome wasn't the cradle of civilization, it was the nursery, et cetera, et cetera. Every time he added a church or museum to their itinerary (espresso and gelato stops were also included), Rachel did her *Dad's a muppet* look, crossing her eyes and jigging her head. She did this discreetly so that only Rowan could see. She was already in an evil mood having discovered she would be missing a friend's thirteenth birthday party in London. The way she saw it, Rome was the obstacle to personal happiness and social success.

The first night had been pleasant enough. After checking into a small hotel near the Piazza del Popolo, they walked all evening until their feet hurt. They saw famous fountains and piazzas, Caravaggio and Raphael, ending the night in Trastevere, gazing up at the firmament of Cavallini mosaics. Just as Rowan crashed into bed—he was sharing a twin room with his sister, giving him an agitating proximity to her bathroom rituals—Rachel told him that she was bored out of her mind and would stab someone if she had to look at another mannerist masterpiece. "FYI, I am not going sightseeing tomorrow—just so you know."

He rolled onto his side to face the wall. "That's not going to happen." He pulled his pillow over his head.

"I'm not"—she jumped on him—"joking."

Rowan bolted upright, "If you don't—" He sacked her with the pillow, lobbed magazines at her—anything to make her go away. He threatened her with the Holy Bible but reconsidered because of the weight. Once she was satisfied that sufficient havoc had been made, Rachel launched herself, cackling, into her own bed.

The next morning, over cornetto and cappuccino in the lobby's *caffè*, Rachel told her family that she had cramps and wasn't well enough to go out.

Michael swallowed his pastry and turned to his wife as the arbiter of all things Rachel. "Is this necessary?" he wanted to know, with barely concealed dismay.

Catherine closed her eyes, something she did when she was stressed, but when she opened them she was eerily calm. "What's the point of making her go if she'll be miserable?"

"Thanks." Rachel grabbed the room key. She was quizzical. She wasn't expecting them to be such pushovers. On the way to the stairs, she glanced back at Rowan to make a mournful face that only he could read was triumph.

"I'd better stay behind as well," their mother added, making her a total accomplice in the matter.

Rowan stared at his parents, agog. He couldn't believe Rachel was being given a free pass for a D- performance. If he had been told to stay in bed to wank, they couldn't have been any more indulgent.

Michael gathered his guidebooks and pamphlets. With a tight smile, he rose from the table, turning to Rowan. "Looks like you are the last man standing." He was grasping for something that approximated ironic humor, but the remark came out heavily and landed with a clunk. Rowan wanted to help his father out by making his words become, in a literal sense, true, so he stood up too. He followed him out of the hotel, leaving his mother still sitting there. She'd put on dark glasses that made her even more inscrutable.

"Have a good time," she called after them. Under the circumstances, she was the one who managed to sound ironic.

His father walked quickly, dodging pedestrians and cars, weaving through the streets to the honk of cars and scooters. There was no breeze, only the heat and steady expulsion of exhaust that seemed a little sweeter baked into ancient stone.

Rowan was slow at first, disoriented by the sudden exposure to the sights and sounds. He felt like a mole, head aboveground, squinting in the daylight—unlike his mother, neither he nor his father had remembered to bring sunglasses. By the time they had climbed all 124 of the Aracoeli steps to the highest point of the Capitoline Hill, they were out of breath and sweating. Seeing that his dad's shirt had become transparent Rowan called a "wet T-shirt competition" and they laughed because it was no contest: Michael's flesh baring through white cotton had already won against the absorbent taupe of a Gap polo. Having put some distance from the scene of disappointment, his father seemed freer and walked with his arms swinging loosely from his shoulders. Inside the Palazzo Nuovo he became expansive, waving at the busts of emperors, introducing them to Rowan as if he were at a party of old friends: *Oh hello, there's Trajan. Marcus Aurelius! Good to see you, my man.* They kicked around on the Via Sacra, deciphering as many tablets as time and skill would allow, and ambled up the Palatine hill to eat stringy rice balls in the shade of an oleander tree. Looking down from the site of Rome's first settlement, they strained to imagine what the valley must have looked like pre-Republic and Empire, when it was a marsh populated by Latin farmers and goats. For all the sights Rowan saw that day, the Roman experience didn't turn him on. Sure, he admired the artistry of Michelangelo and Bernini, but he was conscious that every major monument marked the overthrow of another: the Campidoglio was conceived for an emperor's triumphal march, the rebuilding of St. Peter's was the ultimate in counter-reformation propaganda; with every step he was treading on the graves of slaves and the overthrown. Standing in the Piazza San Pietro under a giant obelisk that had been carried from Alexandria at the whim of Caligula, it spooked him to think that before it was placed there it had also shadowed the psycho-barbarism of Nero's games. As peace was a blink on the timeline and war was the constant, he wondered what would happen next in this piazza of pilgrims, tourists, and hawkers. Up on Palatine he had started wondering what tangible social benefit there had been from building these massive, fuck-off cities—apart from making better water and sewer systems to combat disease. Obviously, the point was to advertise the glory and culture of the ruling classes, but there had always been too many people and not enough places to live. He didn't like the way elaborate architecture was used to screen and barrier reality.

Rowan returned to the hotel to find Rachel, miserable in the room.

"Where did you go?" her voice quavered with reproach. "I tried phoning but you didn't answer."

"Out. You said you weren't coming." He'd left his phone switched off in his backpack, which he hadn't thought to bring.

"I changed my mind. You didn't wait long."

"You know what Dad's like. *Best foot forward . . .*"

"I came down almost immediately. I went outside to find you and these creeps came up jabbering *che cosa fai.* I didn't know which way you had gone, so I had to come back here."

"Didn't Mum tell you we'd left?"

"She couldn't, duh, if she was with you."

This was a point of discussion at dinner when they worked out that Mum had gone to her own room seconds before Rachel had come down. Apparently, she didn't want to disturb Rachel but had left her all day in the room to rest. Privately, Rachel admitted to Rowan that she had regretted not going with them. It had been depressing in the room. There was nothing on TV and she'd found a spider in the sink. She admitted to feeling guilty that she hadn't made more effort for Dad with all his *muppet arrangements*.

Looking back on the weekend from the perspective of the tennis court, he could see how it prefigured the future. Everything Rachel had done was a tryout for an event that never happened, with the result hanging there, a jammed scoreboard that he would thump to move along the result if he could. That she liked winding everyone up was a given, but for what purpose he would never really know. Plus, there was another question lodged there unanswered: why, for all her stuff, did she never con him? She was always honest about lying. When things started happening with boyfriends and partying—the false-alarm pregnancy—she always told him what was going on, even though he didn't want to know. Often, he felt she was trying to pull him into something that wasn't his; maybe she was trying to bring him down with her, because she was going that direction, fast. He went with her some of the way because he was curious and willing, until he balked. Her parties at the house when his mum and dad were away at Hamdean, full of buzzed and puking strangers, repelled him, just as the drunken gropes with Char Nestor or Mira, whoever was foisted on him, left him cold. But now he saw another explanation for why she wanted him around. It was the same reason that he'd started having dreams about her when she was still alive: the dreams about the tent he couldn't put up to save his fucking life; the tent he couldn't put up to save hers. She looked to him to protect her against herself.

Earlier, when he had kissed his father goodbye he had known that it was a significant parting, maybe a final one. His dad's shiny eyes and salty cheeks told him that he was also reckoning with this possibility. But Rowan saw that there would be another goodbye. He would also say *adios* to the comfortable perception that as family referee, chill observer, he hadn't really been involved—when, of course, he was. His sister had looked to him for help and he was implicated. If there was a punishment for denial, it was stabbing clarity. Understanding this was to complete a final crossing, to reach the other side, the place where the adults roamed.

The stone biting into the back of his head was making inroads into his skull and would penetrate all the way through if he allowed. He pushed his head harder into the ground and the pain radiated into his neck, but it wasn't completely excruciating as the temperature of the granite cooled his heated brain.

Fuck!

Skype session with Justice—

Oh shit!

It was coming up soon.

JusticeI had messaged him, *We are not noise, we are happening.*

These words had spoken to him directly and couldn't be denied.

He pushed himself up on his elbows. The relief was instant.

He picked the gravel from the back of his head and inspected the stone. The tip was bloody and sharp as a fang.

He threw it away.

Being a Vitruvian Man wasn't realistic for a basic human, but striving to be *evolutionary smart* was still a reasonable goal.

atherine rose early to see the dawn. She threw on an old skirt, shirt, and tennis shoes and left the house through the French doors of the boiler room. Since hearing the girl describe the living area as a dungeon of a boiler room, no décor, structural innovation, or stuffed sofa, could distract her from thinking of it as one.

Outside, the air was fresh and moist with a recent evaporation of mist. All was still except for the lone chirrup of a bird. Only at this time of the morning, before the day made its disturbances, was nature this pure and serene. As she walked, tendrils of grass caught her bare calves; the dripping flowers of a laburnum brushed past her cheek. Everywhere she looked the leaves and trees had a dewy clarity that was both soft and vivid. The sun was rising behind the hawthorns to make a halo glow of light. Dusk and dawn were known as *magic hour*. In that moment, the beginning of the day didn't seem so much an enchantment as mystical and divine.

She was unusually calm. She had relapsed into sadness the day before, and spent most of it in her bedroom crying. She had cried for Rachel. Cried for Rowan. She'd had moments of compassion thinking about the girl, ruing that the past must have caught up with her poor, damaged soul. *"It always does. You can only be so brave."* She spared some tears for herself, for the days when she'd had purpose and belonged to the world. She belonged to no one.

"You have to have to be of use to belong."

She was a little better today. She was already becoming reconciled to Rowan's brave new world even if she wasn't part of it. Michael had convinced her that resistance would be futile. She had no choice but to embrace their new reality. Surrendering didn't come naturally; yielding went against her instinct to fight. Once done, it was liberating. Submission was a new experience that laid her open to another perspective, where she could entertain the positive, look to the future, see that it might not be as bleak as she had supposed. Perhaps she was wrong not to have more confidence in Rowan. Perhaps he was on the path to greatness. He might become the voice of his generation; the galvanic force behind environmental revolution. In the meantime, she had artists and a husband to nurture. Michael was right about selling Hamdean, right to suggest that she go to London this week. This was all possible. This was all something she could do.

There was movement in the undergrowth by the laurels. When the developer partitioned the house, a line of laurels was planted to mark the boundary between front and back. The trees had grown slowly and plateaued at a dwarfish three feet.

It was Judith! She was practically on all fours, foraging. Really, the woman was extraordinary. *"A veritable sedge pig!"*

Judith looked up. "Catherine!" she called out brightly. "You're up with the larks." She rose to her feet, waving a bunch of nettles in her gloved hand. "Will you come have tea after your walk?"

"Will do." Catherine waved back

"I'd like to talk to you about the banging . . ."

"Yes, yes, of course," Catherine said, with no intention of going. *Always imposing. What right does she have to intrude?* She was drawn toward the remains of the old summerhouse, the remains of the place where the beautiful people used to go. The area wasn't easy to find. If she hadn't known it was there, she might have passed it by. The concrete foundation was only visible in patches, steadily reclaimed by nature, inch by inch, covered with tufts of grass. A robin flew down, hopped on the gray fragments. With a quiver, it took flight, as if it had been frightened away.

Someone was there.

Catherine turned and saw the girl standing by the house. From what she could tell from a distance, the girl was watching her with a blank stare. Her lack of affect was disconcerting. Catherine wasn't sure if she wanted to be with her alone. Although she had shunned Judith before, suddenly the idea of her company wasn't so undesirable. She looked to her neighbor for support, but Judith was gone.

The girl began walking towards her.

Catherine took a deep breath and tried to remember why she

had wanted to see her. After so many weeks of wondering and waiting, the girl had come back as she had hoped she would. She had asked for her return, and here she was alive and safe. Safe and alive. Wasn't this all that mattered? Until she had been given a chance to give her account of whatever happened with Lewis's friend, Hetty, or Betty, it was only fair to suspend judgment and be open minded; it was possible Letty was culpable in the relationship. Even if the girl was guilty of all that Lewis had said, it was important to make peace with her, if only to give the relationship closure. After reminding herself of these simple values, the suspicion she had harbored was displaced with a heart-swelling gladness.

The girl moved slowly. She seemed in no hurry to reach her, giving Catherine the chance to look at her again.

Her eyes were smaller than she remembered, and her mouth curved down at the edges. Her expression was both sullen and dull, as if an internal light had been switched off.

Catherine's enthusiasm dimmed accordingly.

When the girl was close enough to hear, Catherine called out: "It would have been nice if you had phoned." As her words were intended to reproach, it maddened her that the girl didn't respond. This provoked her to go forward and pull back the girl's lapel.

As expected, there were still price tags inside.

"This doesn't belong to you." Catherine said, releasing her jacket in disgust. "You've probably taken from me too, but I'm too addled to have noticed."

The girl gazed insouciantly back, as if she knew she had been found out but didn't care.

Catherine wanted to slap her.

"There was a summerhouse here," she continued. "I saw a photograph. You must have remembered. I don't believe you forgot. I want to know why you bothered to lie. Think before you answer—you might as well be truthful. I mean, apart from me, who else cares a shit?"

"Oh, hello, Keira. How are you?" the girl said, strolling past. "I'm well." She answered her own question. "*Thanks very much for asking.*"

She sauntered toward the remains of the old gazebo. On her feet were black ballet-style pumps that were collapsed at the sides. As soon as she reached the foundations, she stopped and tapped the hard surface with her right toe.

"Since you ask," she said, "here it is—voilà . . ." She had an elegant point and used it to trace a circle. "It doesn't look much now, does it? Considering this was the pinnacle of my mother's existence." She eyed the concrete fragment sardonically. "This was built as a stage for her, somewhere she could go to dance, *express herself*—although I never saw her use it for anything other than hanging out and drinking with friends—it was basically an open-air party place. There used to be candles, rugs and cushions, scattered about . . ."

"They were all out here that night. My mother was with Elise, who was also a dancer. If you thought my mother was beautiful, Elise was more. I don't know why my mother let her go anywhere near my father. Maybe she was using her as bait to lure him back, or maybe she was infatuated with her too. Everyone was drunk. The Stones were playing on a boombox—

'Sympathy for the Devil.' The women were dancing together. They let me run between them, calling me *firefly*, twirling me around until I was giddy. I remember thinking how hip and sophisticated I was, to stay up late and be included. Then someone had the idea that the view on the roof would be incredible and the party moved up there. By then they had forgotten about me and didn't notice that I was following. They just clambered on, loaded—the whole lot of them were plastered.

"It's true, the view up there is amazing. When you're up that high you can see for miles. Once it was totally dark it was trippy, you couldn't tell where the roof ended and the sky began. There was more dancing, more drinking, I saw my mother kissing another man—Elise was all over my father. A row erupted. My mother was shrieking at Elise and she backed away. As there were no railings or walls, she just stood back and dropped off the edge into the darkness. I had been hiding behind a vent and I ran downstairs to bed. I think I heard someone call after me. There was a clamor. Voices. I stayed awake as long as I could, but eventually I fell asleep. The next morning at breakfast everyone was wearing dark glasses. Elise wasn't there and no one said anything more about her. It was as if she had never existed. Not long after I was sent to stay with my cousin and I never saw my father again."

"My God, poor child. What a terrible secret to carry," Catherine cried. "Did you talk to anyone about this?"

"Who was I to tell? The point is, I don't know what I saw that night. *It might have all been a dream.*"

She had a sense of foreboding as she climbed the stairs. She didn't want to go, but having asked the question, she had committed herself to hearing an answer and was obliged to proceed. The girl went first as she knew the way, although it made Catherine very uncomfortable to be led through her own house by someone she no longer liked or trusted, and knew even less than she'd wanted to believe.

They went to the top floor, the attic that she and Michael had taken pains to convert to make bedrooms for the children. It was a dusty spider trap once, a web of exposed beams, but after the ceiling had been raised, wood glossed with paint, and every other surface wallpapered and carpeted, it had become as comfortable as any country-house hotel.

Lush! Love it, Mum, Rachel had said when she saw the finished room. She'd patted her mother's shoulders, an aborted hug, before turning to explore the new decor. Catherine could have taken her in her arms to show her the way, but that would have been risky: Rachel could be prickly, and Catherine wasn't demonstrative—they were not ones for physical affection. Rachel never had the chance to make the bedroom her own, having stayed there only twice. She left a toweling sweatshirt behind the door, and a rosary of carved wooden beads that Michael had given her years before, after coming back from a day's sightseeing in Rome. At the time, Catherine hadn't fully registered the gift, thinking it a tourist trinket that would get rubbished on her bedroom floor along with all her other things. Evidently it had more significance that Rachel had brought it with her. It was only after the girl had stayed at Hamdean that Catherine had ventured farther upstairs and realized it was there. When she told Michael about the presence of the rosary in her bedroom (like her, he hadn't been in since the accident), he went directly to look. The sight of the beads draped across Rachel's dressing-table mirror had made him break down and cry.

Her failure to imagine that Rachel might have appreciated her father's token wasn't the only moment that Catherine had been out of sync with her family that day. During the week prior to the holiday in Rome, Rachel had bleated and complained about leaving London. It came as no surprise when Rachel was suddenly indisposed to go out the morning after their arrival. Catherine didn't have the patience to parlay this challenge into a learning moment. Instead, she let her family to do what they all wanted and had walked out of the hotel to do the same. Her destination was the Church of Santa Maria della Vittoria to see the *Ecstasy of St. Teresa*, a luminous marble beauty that John Bramley had once told her that she must visit one day. Bernini's St. Teresa was a preternatural feat of sculpting. Entered by the Holy Spirit in the form of an angel's arrow, St. Teresa reclined in rapture, gripped by paroxysms not entirely spiritual while her robes manifested sensation in a turbulent sea of waves. That Catherine had left her family to commune with this sensual work that her dead friend, already gone too long, had wanted her to see, was transgressive, defiant, yet ridiculously easy. In furthering her desires, she believed that she was making a stand for herself against the sometimes mind-numbing aspects of parenting. Her mother's example was always there in the background as a warning: she had given herself entirely to her family, yet it had done her no good. If Catherine was more like her than she wanted to admit, withholding was fine too: there was less chance of inflicting damage on her unsuspecting family. Or so she thought. She regretted it all. What she wouldn't give to have that day again, to fill it with messy love and frustration.

We think we have unlimited time. But we don't, and so we squander . . .

They were outside Rachel's door but Catherine kept walking. She didn't want to draw attention to Rachel's room in case the girl asked to go in there.

At the far end of the landing there was a retractable wooden ladder and a trapdoor in the vaulted ceiling. The opening had been pointed out by the estate agent during their first viewing, but Catherine had never had the wherewithal to pull down the steps and discover where they led.

Keira pressed forward and mounted the ladder. With her

arms shaking above her head, she pushed up the hatch, enabling Catherine to follow her as she climbed up and out onto the roof.

Braced by a cool wind, Catherine turned on her heels, 360 degrees. The view was tremendous. Apart from an unexpectedly pretty patchwork of golf course, and the occasional converted oast on the margins of the village, the Weald was untouched by urban development; the land, as green and pleasant as it had been at the time of Blake's poem and the writing of the hymn. At first the sights thrilled and enervated her, but soon they were vertiginous. The height and exposure was dizzying.

She checked her footing. It wasn't bad, although a little uneven. The roof was leaded with odd castellated vents rising up, and many stacked chimneys, some of which couldn't be seen from the ground. She couldn't figure out where they all went. She quickly counted six chimneys on her side of the house, and that didn't include the part belonging to Judith and the mysterious accountant. Catherine had three fireplaces; this meant another three had been made redundant, blocked one by one as the needs of former occupants dictated.

"I'm surprised you haven't been up here. Do you know your husband has? He loves these vistas."

Her comment was jarring. Inappropriately familiar coming from someone Michael had never met. How would she even know that when Catherine didn't know he'd been up there herself?

"A view like this can clear your mind, free you from your cares below." She stated, a touch of parody in her voice.

That was definitely something Michael might have said.

With a thump in her chest, Catherine realized she must have met Michael, and if she had they must have met in secret.

My God, had she seduced him as well?

That thought was quickly followed by another: that she was after Rowan. She was behind Rowan's sudden interest in his bequest. The night she stayed she must have rifled Catherine's files and found out about his money. There was no way Rowan would have discovered by himself. He was always the most unworldly, unmaterialistic child. He never even liked getting birthday presents.

"You'll go through his money in no time. You'll end up living in a yurt in the Hebrides. You'll freeze."

The girl seemed to think this was funny. "That's a very strange thing to say." She smirked, pulling a pack of cigarettes from her pocket. Lighting up, she took a drag.

"Rowan should stay in school." Catherine was adamant. She couldn't help saying of the cigarette: "That'll kill you."

A cloud of smoke curled over her lips. "If life doesn't first," the girl said, exhaling.

Catherine wanted the girl to go but the question was, would she ever leave? Her mind raced through the options. She could pay her off. That was the most likely solution for a venal operator. They were always short of cash but she could give her the Bramley painting of Sutton Hoo, worth over two hundred grand, her most valuable portable asset, a postmodern masterwork. The girl would sell it, but then she'd be gone . . .

"You'd have to give me more than a picture of cabbages."

Catherine stiffened. This girl had calculated everything.

She knew the value of the picture. She knew the value of what was left of her family. But that wasn't enough. She wanted more. "They are not cabbages," she corrected sharply.

"You hate me now, don't you?"

Again, her perception was accurate. Catherine didn't deny it. The disappointment was bitter but not entirely surprising. Hadn't she known from the beginning that this girl would disappoint? Wasn't this always part of her charm?

Catherine watched her sashay to the farthest point south, where the roof levels dropped ten feet, and the eighteenth century lorded over the seventeenth century. Circling to the north, she stopped where the roof was flattest and open and there was the best view of the land.

"Have you ever seen classical dancers jive to rock? They're so wooden and awkward it's hilarious, yet they have bodies that make every pose divine. It's funny because when you meet them they seem larger than life, arresting, but if you try to get to know them or pin them down, they're like vapor."

"Is that why you came? To find out what happened?"

"I came because I heard about a woman who lived in a big house who thought she had everything, but it turned out that she had nothing. She had lost everything along the way because she hadn't loved her family enough. And I thought, That place sounds familiar. Must see if anything has changed. I might get lucky."

Catherine wasn't sure what happened next because she went toward the girl. If she was honest, there was anger in her heart and the girl might have mistaken this for intent. The girl took several steps back. As she had described before, there was no wall or barrier.

She fell silently away.

Whether she had fallen by accident or whether she had jumped because the will to go was greater than the will to stay, Catherine couldn't say.

How long Catherine remained outside before Judith found her and sounded the alarm she didn't know. That was left to the police and experts to try to determine.

atherine had been in the shade longer than she had realized. The sun had bowed down behind the roof. With the sinking orb, the temperature had dropped as well. She moved her wrists and ankles to bring circulation back to her stiffening limbs. The cold seemed to have penetrated her bones. The forensic investigators worked with increased urgency and seemed to have accelerated their pace, as if they knew that with the fading light they were running out of time. Catherine was drawn to them, curious to know what they had discovered— one of them had tweezers and was putting something that looked like a cigarette butt into a plastic bag. She was interested to see what they had found.

She didn't want to be alone.

As the workers neared, they moved politely aside, much as the archeologists had done that day at Sutton Hoo. She was grateful that she was being treated with respect, as one of them, not as a guilty party or dreadful perp.

I wouldn't be lying if I told them that she moved in on us at a bad time.

Judith was wandering around, her crochet shawl trailing behind her on the ground. One of her braids had come undone, giving her a lopsided air. She was crying, a lost child with a blankie. She no longer looked beatific or particularly beautiful, but stark raving batty.

The sky seemed to dim and lower over strands of bleeding gold. Somewhere in the distance, Catherine could hear the rhythmic chirp of a robin. It was the whistle and squeak of her father's wheelbarrow on the way to the dump as he journeyed to make beauty and art. Underneath, she heard a more melodious warble, a figured bass.

What color is that?

She was talking to her father about his first bell krater.

You tell me, Catherine.

It's not red or orange exactly, she answered. *It's burning. Like Saturn. Or the rays of the sun before it goes down?*

I couldn't have put better myself, dear girl. That is true.

She was confused because she could no longer see the vase, nor the bench, nor the wisteria. The tent seemed to have risen around her while she lay, helpless, on the ground, watching herself be enveloped.

This was strange.

She would have liked to complain, as she'd wanted when the spaceman had rudely trampled her daffs, but even then, with each passing second, the desire to protest seemed to wane. The man who had interviewed her before was leaning over with his face intimately close to hers. She could have kissed him if she had been able to turn her head. She realized that she could no longer move her neck or body. She was frozen. Physical sensation was ebbing away, but not so much that she couldn't feel the pressure in her temples; that her eyes were swollen and might soon burst and overflow; and that if that were to happen there was nothing she could do to wipe them clear.

That was a pity.

She would have liked to cry, to wish Michael by her side.

But that wasn't possible.

Judith sobbed, "I saw her out here this morning, talking to herself . . . banging, banging, banging, every night on the walls. I should have known."

"Is there anything you would like to say?" the man whispered in Catherine's ear.

"You won't get anything from her now. She's almost gone," someone answered instead.

If she'd still had words, she would have told him to make sure that Michael understood that Rowan was all right because he mustn't be allowed to think, even for a second, that anything had happened to their son. The jangle of the BlackBerry was always a reminder that disaster was one phone call away. Whenever the phone rang, there was always an awful pause before one of them would say, *I'll get it.* That was something he should never have to experience again.

She would have liked to tell Michael that she loved him more than she'd understood, that her infatuation with John Bramley, her ridiculous, special relationship, was only a heightened mutuality, a form of self-regard or narcissism. It was nothing compared to the grist and substance of their years together.

Or maybe it was best that she couldn't. Michael wasn't aware of her petty betrayals.

She wasn't sure what she would have said about the girl.

That she was slippery and dangerous?

She came once or twice.

Or not at all?

She did me in all over again when she left.

Up on the roof she had appeared to her so tangible, that at any moment she could have reached out to slap or stroke her pale cheek. Yet, with her final stirrings of consciousness, the awareness that she, not the girl, had made the sheer plunge down, the illusion of certainty dissolved as she was pulled along stream by the current, to the sea.

She wasn't leaving but swimming. The water was ultramarine and welcoming—she had already heard that the temperature was warm. She would swim to her mother, swim to Rachel and keep going until all that held her were the waves.

Rachel was happy the night before she died. When Rachel's small effects were returned, Catherine looked at the last photograph taken on her daughter's phone. Rachel was in a swimming pool, leaping up from the water like a dolphin, arms outstretched with an expression of unbelievable joy.

The heat was searing.

It was better than the chill.

The previous day, Catherine had driven into town, to a camping store. She had purchased a sleeping bag for Rowan, and had it sent to him at school. It was the best Primaloft, cocoon sack that money could buy.

He would need it for the cold nights of protest ahead.

The children were bantering again. She liked the way they looked out for each other. Rowan was telling his sister about his dream: "The radiators were leaking oil. We'd borrowed Mum's rugs. I was freaking out. It was traumatic."

Haha!

Rachel's laughter was

Why don't you come   with?

water

warm

Mira is here in a sexy bikini ?

??

Answer me!

Your such a prick!

Ro?

u will always b 2 Yz for me.

M ichael liked to stay late in the office after most of his colleagues had gone home. The din of construction outside had stopped and the telephone didn't ring, leaving him free to concentrate on whatever loose ends needed tying up on his desk. Having cleared his head of aberrant thoughts about Paige, which were exactly that, a test of who he was and what he wanted, he was able to finish looking over the paperwork for the Horsemead Estate. It would have been neglectful to leave the contract unread any longer.

As a child Michael always had fantastical dreams. This was, in part, because his father had fostered an interest in history by telling him stories from Greek and Roman mythology. From his father—later, his own readings—he learned of capricious gods, multiheaded monsters, and incestuous mothers. These tales worked on his imagination and gave him license to find adventure away from a home that was devoid of drama or conflict, where nothing much happened beyond the pages of

Homer, or the outgrowing of a pair of shoes. At night, Michael became Odysseus, hurtling in his bark on the crest of a wave, or fighting his way out of a Cyclops's cave. In his dreams, he was as brave as Theseus. He strode unarmed into battle to mediate a truce between Achilles and Hector. For his courage, he was carried on men's shoulders and hailed *Michael Francis, Peacemaker of Troy*. With his incarnations not just limited to noble fighters and demigods—there was a memorably hairy one when he was a donkey on a sacrificial altar—the triumph wasn't always in his heroism but that in critical moments of danger he could wake himself up by saying, *Everything is going to be all right*, with these words acting as a spell to grant him release and bring him safely back to consciousness. For the last fourteen months, he had walked with Catherine in darkness. There were no words to charm death, nor an Apollo to raise them up to heaven from the underworld. Rowan had emerged as a guide. Much as a prayer, his son's example had worked on him, making him alive to the holiness of existence. Seeing him on the weekend had been a waking spell from the perpetual night of Rachel's death.

On Sunday morning, he had repacked his overnight bag before driving to London. He had asked Catherine to go with him. She had hesitated; then refused. Something made him ask, "You are not waiting for that girl to come back, are you?"

"No," Catherine replied. "Not anymore."

Just as he was leaving, she'd said, "You'll always be all right. All you have to do is be yourself and keep walking." This had struck him as odd, but he had accepted the remark as an off-centered compliment. He had crossed to the bed, where she still lay naked under the sheets. He kissed her on the cheek, which he remembered afterward had been clammy. "Point is to walk together . . . Come to London this week?"

She tilted her head slightly and pouted slightly. He used to tease her that she did that when she was thinking. "We'll see."

The message light on the office landline was still flashing. It was the missed call from Hamdean. He couldn't delay playing it any longer.

He took a deep breath and told himself:

Everything is going to be all right.

Everything is going to be all right.

Acknowledgments

Heartfelt thanks to: my editor, Jill Bialosky, whose suggestions, intelligence, and empathy shaped this book; my agent, Sarah Chalfant, for her staunch support and tireless belief; Rebecca Nagel at the Wylie Agency; the editorial and production teams at W. W. Norton; Hilton Als, who guided me through the drafts; Ann Biderman, Michelle Hunevan, and Becky Johnston, for their invaluable comments on the manuscript; Holly Goldberg Sloan; Yassi Mazandi, who shared her knowledge of clay; stalwart early readers Annette Bening, Rabia Cebeci, Cressida Connolly, Grace Griesbach, J. Leigh, Paul Lister, Brian Siberell, Maura Swanson, Suzanne Tenner, Susan Traylor, for their wisdom and the oxygen of friendship; Julian, Natalya and Imogen, for the ineffable joy and wonder.

THE SHADES

Evgenia Citkowitz

THE SHADES
Evgenia Citkowitz

DISCUSSION QUESTIONS

1. The point of view in *The Shades* continually switches between Catherine, Michael, and Rowan, allowing the reader access to the intimate thoughts of each character. How does this help to build a picture of the events surrounding Rachel's death? How does the structure create tension? What insights can be gained from each character's grieving process?

2. In the first chapter, Catherine balks at the sight of the forensic investigator trampling on her daffodils. She thinks about "the need after a disaster to preserve what was left" (p. 14). Is this instinct borne out by any of the characters in the book? How?

3. To what extent is Rowan's desire to leave school to fight climate change a reaction to his sister's death?

4. Michael and Catherine have vastly different reactions to the poem Rowan reads at Rachel's funeral (p. 57). How are their reactions indicative of their relationships with both Rowan and Rachel?

5. Michael's courtship of Catherine does not go well until he takes her to see *L'Orfeo* (pp. 26–27). After the opera, she is more willing to give Michael a chance. What is it about Catherine's experience that causes her to change her mind? How does the mythology of the opera resonate through *The Shades*?

6. Rachel looms large throughout the narrative. How does the author build a portrait of her character?

7. How does Catherine's attitude toward Keira change over the course of the story? What does this shifting perception reveal about Catherine? Catherine is the only character to encounter Keira—do you feel that her accounts of Keira are always reliable?

8. How would you explain what happened to Catherine on the roof at the end of the novel? Did you question Catherine's reality at any point? What do you think Catherine finally understands at the end?

9. Is Keira's visit to Hamdean a catalyst for Catherine's fate? Does Catherine's desperate desire and inability to help the young woman in a way she couldn't help Rachel factor into what happens?

10. What is the significance of the novel's title?

11. Before Michael listens to the message from Hamdean he tells himself, "Everything is going to be all right" (p. 197). How do these words embody Michael's character? Do you feel these lines are knowing, or signify hope in any way?

12. Art plays a significant role in the novel. Catherine's father was an artisan, shaping pieces out of clay in his studio. Catherine owns an art gallery and is reputed for her eye. Rowan creates a cuff that is placed on exhibition at his school. How are questions about the value of art and creativity woven with the question of identity? How does art foreshadow events at the end of the book?

13. *The Shades* examines the grief of a family after losing a daughter and sister. Citkowitz uses a deft hand when addressing the subject. When is the theme of grief most potent, and when is it most subtle?

14. The penultimate chapter is a continuation of the opening of the book, as told from Catherine's perspective. After reading *The Shades*, how has your understanding of what took place at the beginning changed?

*Available only on the Norton website